**ANTAC**

**VOL. 1**

© 2021 Marcus V. Calvert

By Tales Unlimited, LLC.

All rights reserved.

No portion of this book may be reproduced in any form without permission from the publisher.

For permissions, contact:
https://www.talesunlimited.net.

Cover by Lincoln Adams

Edited by Ed Buchanan

## Acknowledgments

*I'd like to thank Ed Buchanan and my beta readers for beating this one into shape.*

*As always, I must salute Lincoln Adams for yet another awesome book cover.*

*Rose, thanks for keeping me in the game.*

*To everyone else who had a hand in this twisted thing being written (living or not), I thank you.*

*I must also tip a hat to my fellow artists and strangers-turned-fans. You truly are a hip crowd.*

# The Antagonists' Cookbook, Vol. 1

| | |
|---|---|
| QUICK INSTRUCTIONS | 12 |
| DETAILED INSTRUCTIONS | 20 |
| Recipe #01 – Acromage Tahini | 25 |
| Recipe #02 – Adrenaline Bandit Wings | 26 |
| Recipe #03 – Alchemical Parmesan | 27 |
| Recipe #04 – Alien Vampire Flakes | 28 |
| Recipe #05 – Almond Hunter-Killer | 29 |
| Recipe #06 – Android Spy Soup | 30 |
| Recipe #07 – Aqua Alien Florentine | 31 |
| Recipe #08 – Aqua Gladiator Stroganoff | 32 |
| Recipe #09 – Aquabeast Cheese Puffs | 33 |
| Recipe #10 – Archer's Curse Stir Fry | 34 |
| Recipe #11 – Armor & Spinach Wrap | 35 |
| Recipe #12 – Armor Sprouts | 36 |
| Recipe #13 – Armored Fae Slaw | 37 |
| Recipe #14 – Assembly Line Guacamole | 38 |
| Recipe #15 – Axe Killer Patties | 39 |
| Recipe #16 – Bacon Spirit Slayer | 40 |
| Recipe #17 – Baked Cyberkiller | 41 |
| Recipe #18 – Bang Bang Armor | 42 |
| Recipe #19 – Basil & Medicine Man | 43 |
| Recipe #20 – Beastie Fettuccine | 44 |
| Recipe #21 – Berry Glacial Nuke | 45 |

| | |
|---|---|
| Recipe #22 – Berserker & Onion | 46 |
| Recipe #23 – Bioslaughter Muffins | 47 |
| Recipe #24 – Blackberry Sword Sleuth | 48 |
| Recipe #25 – Blended Eye Beamer | 49 |
| Recipe #26 – Blind Boss Mushroom | 50 |
| Recipe #27 – Bok Choy Grifter | 51 |
| Recipe #28 – Boss Armor Melon Bowl | 52 |
| Recipe #29 – Boss Pad Thai | 53 |
| Recipe #30 – Bound Djinn Sweet Roll | 54 |
| Recipe #31 – Brainwash Veal | 55 |
| Recipe #32 – Brainwasher Sauté | 56 |
| Recipe #33 – Bratwurst Mole Implant | 57 |
| Recipe #34 – Breaded Demon Spy | 58 |
| Recipe #35 – Broiled Mentor | 59 |
| Recipe #36 – Broken Alignment Medley | 60 |
| Recipe #37 – Brute Broth | 61 |
| Recipe #38 – Brutish Enchilada | 62 |
| Recipe #39 – Caramel Volley | 63 |
| Recipe #40 – Cat Burglar Deluxe | 64 |
| Recipe #41 – Chestnut Researcher | 65 |
| Recipe #42 – Chicken Ranch Figment | 66 |
| Recipe #43 – Child Sleuth Sardines | 67 |
| Recipe #44 – Chilled Pen Pal | 68 |

# The Antagonists' Cookbook, Vol. 1

| | |
|---|---|
| Recipe #45 – Cinnamon Stuck | 69 |
| Recipe #46 – Coconut Witch Hunter | 70 |
| Recipe #47 – Combat Telekinetic Bread | 71 |
| Recipe #48 – Copycat Pancakes | 72 |
| Recipe #49 – Corrupt Speedster Bites | 73 |
| Recipe #50 – Creamy Super Spy | 74 |
| Recipe #51 – Crisped Power Thief | 75 |
| Recipe #52 – Cryo Villain Chutney | 76 |
| Recipe #53 – Cucumber Prankster | 77 |
| Recipe #54 – Curried Luck Demigod | 78 |
| Recipe #55 – Curse Fist Soup | 79 |
| Recipe #56 – Cyber Stretch Pasta | 80 |
| Recipe #57 – Cyberwing Beef Bowl | 81 |
| Recipe #58 – Death Demigod Omelet | 82 |
| Recipe #59 – Death's Minion Loaf | 83 |
| Recipe #60 – Demon Brawler Blintz | 84 |
| Recipe #61 – Demon Crooner Dip | 85 |
| Recipe #62 – Demon Rider Licorice | 86 |
| Recipe #63 – Deviled Stench | 87 |
| Recipe #64 – Devil's Advocate Salsa | 88 |
| Recipe #65 – Dipped Dragon Daddy | 89 |
| Recipe #66 – Drone Soufflé | 90 |
| Recipe #67 – Drunken Kielbasa | 91 |

| | |
|---|---|
| Recipe #68 – Dutch Apple Hexter | 92 |
| Recipe #69 – Earth Elemental Tacos | 93 |
| Recipe #70 – Earthquake Pudding | 94 |
| Recipe #71 – Elemental Warrior Mousse | 95 |
| Recipe #72 – Euphoria Sandwich | 96 |
| Recipe #73 – Executioner Pie | 97 |
| Recipe #74 – Face-Lift Marinara | 98 |
| Recipe #75 – Fallen Elf Chips | 99 |
| Recipe #76 – Feta Spinach Acolyte | 100 |
| Recipe #77 – Fire Elemental Bologna | 101 |
| Recipe #78 – Fortune-Teller Sundae | 102 |
| Recipe #79 – Fried Crystal Monster | 103 |
| Recipe #80 – Frostbite Sorbet | 104 |
| Recipe #81 – Frosted Memory Scholar | 105 |
| Recipe #82 – Glazed Enforcer | 106 |
| Recipe #83 – Gluten Free Saboteur | 107 |
| Recipe #84 – Gooey Monster Fudge | 108 |
| Recipe #85 – Ground Starship | 109 |
| Recipe #86 – Hazelnut Psi-Pill Addict | 110 |
| Recipe #87 – Henchperson Noodles | 111 |
| Recipe #88 – Herbal Phasic Sumo | 112 |
| Recipe #89 – Hive Kebab | 113 |
| Recipe #90 – Homestyle Death Blow | 114 |

# The Antagonists' Cookbook, Vol. 1

| | |
|---|---|
| Recipe #91 – Iceform Parfait | 115 |
| Recipe #92 – Imposter Steak | 116 |
| Recipe #93 – Imposter Waffles | 117 |
| Recipe #94 – Instigator Bisque | 118 |
| Recipe #95 – Jalapeño Battle Nun | 119 |
| Recipe #96 – Jellied Atlantean Exile | 120 |
| Recipe #97 – Joke Yogurt | 121 |
| Recipe #98 – Jungle Lord Vampire & Cheese | 122 |
| Recipe #99 – Kidnapper Tiramisu | 123 |
| Recipe #100 – Lemon Glyph Armor | 124 |
| Recipe #101 – Lettuce-Wrapped Cyberspeedster | 125 |
| Recipe #102 – Lime Murder Diva | 126 |
| Recipe #103 – Low-Fat Bone Claw | 127 |
| Recipe #104 – Macaroni & Critter | 128 |
| Recipe #105 – Mad Sender Skillet | 129 |
| Recipe #106 – Magno Armor Pakora | 130 |
| Recipe #107 – Manipulator Goulash | 131 |
| Recipe #108 – Marinated Sentry | 132 |
| Recipe #109 – Mastermind Meringue Pie | 133 |
| Recipe #110 – Meatball Minion | 134 |
| Recipe #111 – Melted Spirit Hustler | 135 |
| Recipe #112 – Metal Burst & Olives | 136 |
| Recipe #113 – Metal Spinner Salmon | 137 |

| | |
|---|---|
| Recipe #114 – Minced Multi-Gunner | 138 |
| Recipe #115 – Mindjacker Teriyaki | 139 |
| Recipe #116 – Mint Combat Alien | 140 |
| Recipe #117 – Miso-Cured Sniper | 141 |
| Recipe #118 – Mixed Alchemical Gadgeteer | 142 |
| Recipe #119 – Mutagenic Slices | 143 |
| Recipe #120 – Mystic Badge Frittata | 144 |
| Recipe #121 – Mystic Gunsmith Pops | 145 |
| Recipe #122 – Oats & Shock Villain | 146 |
| Recipe #123 – Open-Faced Sand Dragon | 147 |
| Recipe #124 – Oven-Fresh Dwarf Rage | 148 |
| Recipe #125 – Pack Smoothie | 149 |
| Recipe #126 – Peaches & Water Elemental | 150 |
| Recipe #127 – Peanut Butter Portal Key | 151 |
| Recipe #128 – Peanut Plant Monster | 152 |
| Recipe #129 – Peas & Cursed Amulet | 153 |
| Recipe #130 – Pecan Cyber Spy | 154 |
| Recipe #131 – Petrification Sausage | 155 |
| Recipe #132 – Phantom Comedian Primavera | 156 |
| Recipe #133 – Phantom Dragon Mix | 157 |
| Recipe #134 – Pheromonal Salami | 158 |
| Recipe #135 – Pickled Doomsday Lair | 159 |
| Recipe #136 – Plant Freak Cheese | 160 |

| | |
|---|---|
| Recipe #137 – Plant Monster S'mores | 161 |
| Recipe #138 – Poached Witch Sniper | 162 |
| Recipe #139 – Power Thief Pancetta | 163 |
| Recipe #140 – Protean Crisp | 164 |
| Recipe #141 – Psi-Rocker Brisket | 165 |
| Recipe #142 – Psi-Teacher Piperade | 166 |
| Recipe #143 – Pureed Blood Sword | 167 |
| Recipe #144 – Raspberry Psi-Vamp | 168 |
| Recipe #145 – Retired Swordsman Squash | 169 |
| Recipe #146 – Rigatoni Support Minion | 170 |
| Recipe #147 – Roasted Bladeshielder | 171 |
| Recipe #148 – Rogue Apprentice Granola | 172 |
| Recipe #149 – Saboteur Liverwurst | 173 |
| Recipe #150 – Sacrificial Weapons Plum | 174 |
| Recipe #151 – Saucy Vampire | 175 |
| Recipe #152 – Sesame Armorer | 176 |
| Recipe #153 – Shadow Broker Chili | 177 |
| Recipe #154 – Shield Sauce | 178 |
| Recipe #155 – Shock Casserole | 179 |
| Recipe #156 – Shock Trooper Rice | 180 |
| Recipe #157 – Singed Pyrokinetic | 181 |
| Recipe #158 – Smoky Pact Killer | 182 |
| Recipe #159 – Sniper Surprise | 183 |

| | |
|---|---|
| Recipe #160 – Sonic Tikka | 184 |
| Recipe #161 – Soul Scalper Alfredo | 185 |
| Recipe #162 – Sourdough Getaway Driver | 186 |
| Recipe #163 – Spaghetti Alpha Vamp | 187 |
| Recipe #164 – Speedster Stew | 188 |
| Recipe #165 – Spell Gangster Danish | 189 |
| Recipe #166 – Split Personality Crepes | 190 |
| Recipe #167 – Scrambled Power Vendor | 191 |
| Recipe #168 – Star God Antipasto | 192 |
| Recipe #169 – Steamed Sisterhood | 193 |
| Recipe #170 – Storm Curry | 194 |
| Recipe #171 – Storm Junkie Saltimbocca | 195 |
| Recipe #172 – Story Dragon Quiche | 196 |
| Recipe #173 – Sugar-Free Gianthood | 197 |
| Recipe #174 – Summoner Fondue | 198 |
| Recipe #175 – Summoner's Puppet Butterscotch | 199 |
| Recipe #176 – Sumo Tots | 200 |
| Recipe #177 – Super Gangster Dumplings | 201 |
| Recipe #178 – Surfer Calzone | 202 |
| Recipe #179 – Tac Vest Gumbo | 203 |
| Recipe #180 – Techie Salad | 204 |
| Recipe #181 – Technopath Au Gratin | 205 |
| Recipe #182 – Telekinetic Basilico | 206 |

| | |
|---|---|
| Recipe #183 – Temporal Gangster Cake | 207 |
| Recipe #184 – Temporal Pocket Rolls | 208 |
| Recipe #185 – Toasted Nanoswarm | 209 |
| Recipe #186 – Tox Shot Assortment | 210 |
| Recipe #187 – Trigger-Happy Venison | 211 |
| Recipe #188 – Tuna Dream Spy | 212 |
| Recipe #189 – Two-Headed Cobbler | 213 |
| Recipe #190 – Undercover Performer Ham | 214 |
| Recipe #191 – Vamp Tarts | 215 |
| Recipe #192 – Vampire Samurai Biscuit | 216 |
| Recipe #193 – Vampiric Crystalline Pie | 217 |
| Recipe #194 – Vegan Sidekick | 218 |
| Recipe #195 – Walnut Demon Blades | 219 |
| Recipe #196 – War Prophet Scampi | 220 |
| Recipe #197 – Whisked Exorcist | 221 |
| Recipe #198 – Whole Grain Techno Dwarf | 222 |
| Recipe #199 – Winged Freak Dijon | 223 |
| Recipe #200 – Zookeeper Pork Pie | 224 |
| ABOUT THE AUTHOR | 225 |
| CURRENT TITLES | 226 |

## QUICK INSTRUCTIONS

Every character has seven attributes: Speed, Endurance, Might, Intellect, Will, Alertness, and Health. Each attribute comes in three levels: human, superhuman, and beyond superhuman.

Super powers (typically) have two levels: superhuman and beyond superhuman.

Any power with a "#" in front of it means that it's a character power (like a killer, genius, alien, etc.).

This book has 200 "Recipes" (or templates) with five "Ingredients" (or super powers) each. These super powers are short, sweet, and flexibly vague. Set them up as you see fit, for whatever story you're out to tell, then fill in the details.

The system works best when you have a general idea of the character you want—from a witch to a psychic to a hostile alien.

To begin, randomly flip to a Recipe page and pick the power(s) best suited for the character type in your head. Jot down the Recipe and Ingredient numbers, then flip to another random page. Repeat the process until you're satisfied. Try not to pick more than five powers—unless you're shooting for a boss-level villain.

Then list them accordingly. *Factor in the attributes and powers—then set the details of both.* Don't be afraid of details. Because the better you know your antagonist(s), the better you know your story.

## SAMPLER ONE:
## A DIFFERENT TYPE OF VAMPIRE

Let's say you wanted to create a different type of alpha vampire.

Put a few of the common traits in your head, like:
*Blood drinking bite
*Physically superior
*Ability to infect others
*A good leader

Stop and flip to that first Recipe. For this example, I ended up at "Recipe #113 – Metal Spinner Salmon." I looked through the (five) Ingredients and found two that I liked:

*4 - #You're a genetic superhuman (born or augmented) with one free power and one superhuman attribute.*

*5 - #You're a super genius with a number of non-violent skill masteries. Boost your Intellect to superhuman capacity.*

For a lesser vamp, I could stop here. I want an alpha though, so I flipped to "Recipe #170 – Storm Curry."

*5 - During a fight, you'll be able to ignore your injuries (from broken bones to fatal wounds) until the fight's over—then it'll all catch up to you. Do note: certain injuries will still kill you on the spot (like decapitation or a nuke blast).*

Impressive—but not quite enough. I flipped pages again and ended up with "Recipe #31 – Brainwash Veal."

*1 - #You're a well-versed killer. Your talents can be merely human or at superhuman capacity.*

*2 - Establish some form of contact and you can alter a target's memories.*

*5 - You can establish two-way, telepathic communications with anyone in your line of sight.*

Now that's an alpha, with six abilities. Time to factor in the attributes, powers, and details.

Being a vampire implies superhuman Speed, Endurance, Might, Alertness, and Health. I'll give the alpha a four-ton lifting capacity. He can't run at MACH speeds or survive a nuke blast. Still, he could tear through a dozen normal humans with ease.

Recipe #113, Ingredient #5 offered him superhuman Intellect. Thus, he would be smart enough to build ultratech gadgets, easily hack into classified networks, or reverse-engineer doomsday weaponry.

Recipe #113, Ingredient #5 also came with a number of free, non-violent skill masteries (to go with the super genius). What are they? I guess it depends on how old the vampire is. Let's say he's fifty-two and only acquired his powers a few years ago, in a lab. Give him degrees in genetics and chemistry. Weapons design and computer networks are his new "hobbies." With that Intellect, he's scary.

Since he's got psychic powers, I gave him a superhuman Will attribute, courtesy of Recipe #113, Ingredient #4. Still, on a good day, a psychic(s) could bring him down.

Recipe #113, Ingredient #4 also came with a free power. Save that one for last. Don't forget that he is a genetic vampire. He intentionally augmented himself. The infectious bite's a biological element (and might even be curable). Also, does he have any weaknesses? Hmm. Let's make him worry about direct sunlight and a vulnerability to poisoned blood.

Then there's Recipe #170, Ingredient #5. Once the fighting starts, a stake to the heart won't kill him. If anything, he'll just rip it out and keep fighting. The protagonist would need poisoned blood, psychics, or damage that he couldn't walk away from (like a beheading).

Recipe #31, Ingredient #1 offers you a chance to define what kind of killer—and adversary—this vamp is. Is he funny or serious? Does he favor a particular killing style? Does he adhere to an ethical code? Being a man of science (and a bit vain), he'll kill most victims without banter or mercy. He might chat with—or even turn—a worthy adversary. Most of his kills are neat and bloodless . . . unless he's hungry.

Recipe #31, Ingredient #2 allows him to play with victims' memories.

Recipe #31, Ingredient #5 provides the means for mental contact.

These two go hand-in-hand. The vampire must sustain a line of sight to edit memories. Also, he cannot read minds.

Now, what's that bonus power (from Recipe #113, Ingredient #4)? The ability to read minds? Unnaturally long life? A paralytic bite? The ability to enter minds from miles away? I'll go with the ability to regenerate.

By the way, cookbook instructions aren't legally binding documents. I could change any of this on a whim. Still, as you can see, the process narrows the possibilities and results in a realistic character with strengths and flaws.

As for this vampire, throw in some nasty aspiration(s) and he looks unbeatable . . . until he runs into your protagonist.

That should make for one heck of a story.

# The Antagonists' Cookbook, Vol. 1

## SAMPLER TWO:
## A DIFFERENT TYPE OF ARTIST

Yep. You read this correctly. What if your urban monster slayer's up against an evil artist? How would that even work? Again, give the artist some basics:

\*A skilled painter
\*Her career's on the rise
\*Something bad happened to her

Now, let's go random. I flipped to "Recipe #120 – Mystic Badge Frittata" and came away with:

*1 - #By day, you're one person. By night, you (literally) morph into someone else. So yeah, generate another character (perhaps even someone without powers).*

Hmm. Didn't see that one coming. It's kind of creepy. Something bad happened to this artist. That pain came out in her earlier works and made her famous.

Her "secret masterpiece" is a comic book diary. In it, she creates a vengeful alter ego to dispatch her enemies. It was supposed to be therapeutic. Yet, at some point, it became real.

I could stop right here . . . Nah. I don't know if this power's mystical or psychic.

I flipped to "Recipe #04 – Alien Vampire Flakes" and picked:

*3 - You can feed on the living, via touch. If your victim's a psychic, then you can hold onto that extra Health until it's removed by damage.*

Two powers are enough for this one—but I'll flip to one last page (just to be sure). I ended up on "Recipe #176 – Sumo Tots" and:

*2 - For better or worse, your name is feared far and wide. Set the pros and cons of having such an infamous rep.*

I'd stop here and start on the attributes, powers, and details.

All seven of the artist's attributes are human-scale. That makes her easy to kill in the daytime. Also, do note that *her two main super powers are both stronger than her mind.* Uh-oh. What if her alter ego's calling the shots—even during the day? Or what if she becomes addicted to feeding on people?

Recipe #91, Ingredient #5 implies one alter ego (that can't be changed). If I was feeling bold, I could allow her to sketch monsters and unleash them into the night.

Nah. Maybe in a later book (hint, hint). For now, I want to play it safe and lock her into one nocturnal character—based on that comic book.

Recipe #04, Ingredient #3 allows for her to feed on minds, via touch. The artist can use this to heal herself, inflict damage to her enemies, enjoy a psychic "high," or maybe even pull off a daytime transformation into her alter ego.

Or, since her Will attribute is so weak, maybe she needs to feed *in order for her transformation to work at all*. What if three normal victims or one psychic were needed to trigger the alter ego? Psychics are especially susceptible to this power and can't resist her touch. To the victim, it's like getting tased, from the inside out. Non-psychics with a superhuman Endurance (or some sort of protection) could fight back.

Maybe the artist got mugged. In a moment of heightened panic, she touched him and fed for the first time. Her Will wasn't strong enough to resist that addictive rush. The human mugger died and his psychic energy was just enough to awaken a voice in her head. It compelled her to feed on two more. Once that was done, she disappeared and the alter ego stood in her place. The more minds she feeds upon, the longer the alter ego can stick around.

Eventually, Recipe #176, Ingredient #2 (the fearsome reputation) would make a lot of sense here—as the bodies continued to pile up.

Okay then, repeat the character generation process and create that avenging entity. Someone (or something) "fun" enough to give that urban monster hunter some serious injuries.

One last thought: what if this artist was the monster hunter's love interest? Or even his kid sister?

## DETAILED INSTRUCTIONS

As previously mentioned, this system comes with 200 "Recipes." Each one is a pre-generated character template. Within each template are five powers that come together (like "Ingredients" in a meal) to create that Recipe.

1. This system works best if you have a vague idea of your antagonist in mind (say, a ninja or witch). Then flip to a random page and find a power(s) that suits that character. Scribble down its Recipe number and Ingredient number(s).

2. Is your character done? If so, stop. If not, flip to another random page. This time, your selections are based on the character and any power(s) already selected. The goal is to create a "whole" character without stacking in too many powers. With each choice, scribble down the Recipe and Ingredient numbers (for future reference).

3. How many powers should a character have? A starting recommendation would be 1-3 powers for a minor character and 4-5 powers for major characters within your story. In the end, it's up to you.

**NOTE: During the generation process, it's okay to replace a selected power(s) if you find something better.**

4. At some point, you'll find a page where none of the powers listed align with your fledgling antagonist. That's fine. You can either continue to another page . . . or treat it as a possible stopping point.

5. The only time I'd recommend going for plenty of powers is if you're designing a genuinely dangerous character. Maybe it's a boss-level super villain, a sentient starship, or a disinterested gambling deity in Chapter Nine of your current novel. The odd thing about this process though? You might be able to destroy the world with *just one power*. Keep that in mind.

6. Try to think up "different" combinations of powers. Stuff people don't see together very often (if ever). Imagine a cursed sword that steals a bit of your morality with every cut. Or a shapeshifting gorgon with a mutagenic bite. With a clever merging of powers, you'll have unforgettable threats for your protagonist.

7. Now, once you've finalized your picks, flesh out the attributes, powers, and details.

8. "Capacity" and "attributes" will be mentioned throughout the power listings. What do they mean?

**CAPACITY:** Think of this as a measure of impact. This system has three capacities (or scales): human, superhuman, and beyond superhuman. A weapon might have a "human" scale (like a knife, sword, or grenade), a "superhuman "scale (like a mystical axe or artillery barrage), or go "beyond superhuman" (like a megaton nuke or a deity's full wrath).

To be clear, superhuman abilities and attributes are beyond those of normal humans. A super genius is smarter than a genius. Someone with superhuman strength can toss cars while a human bodybuilder can't. Going "beyond superhuman" means that an ability has been boosted to freakish levels—even among superhumans. A beyond superhuman skill means that you're impossibly good at something, to the point where it is a power in itself.

**NOTE: The only time a super power should be in the human scale is if it's barely functioning (perhaps because of a power negation device, an adversary's curse, etc.).**

**ATTRIBUTES:** This system has seven attributes for each character:

Speed – How fast/agile/precise you are.

Endurance – How long you can function without sustenance or rest. It's also a measure of pain tolerance.

Might – How strong you are. If you want to put a maximum lifting capacity to a character's strength, suit yourself. Superhuman capacity starts where maximum human capacity ends. Beyond superhuman starts wherever you want it to (100 tons, 1,000 tons, etc.).

Intellect – How smart you are.

Will – Mental strength and resilience.

Alertness – How perceptive you are.

Health – How much damage your body can handle before you die.

> **NOTE: The difference between Endurance and Health is a peculiar one. Someone with a superhuman Endurance (but a human-scale Health attribute) has mad stamina, a great pain tolerance, but might die from a well-placed wound. Now flip this around. Someone with human Endurance and superhuman Health would tire quickly, have a glass jaw, but could still survive an obscene amount of damage.**

Unless you're creating a superhuman character (like an alpha vampire), assume that all starting characters have human-scale attributes. If you want to boost them later (as a tweak), feel free. But at the beginning, treat them like regular people: then give them powers and see what changes.

### IN CONCLUSION . . .

Whether setting up a fight scene, designing weaponry, or cooking up sub-races for a fantasy series, the *Antagonists' Cookbook* will save you a ton of time and wrong turns. This system will help you create intriguing enemies for that awesome hero(ine) of yours.

Lastly, should you use this guide to create your protagonist? **No. Never. <u>A protagonist should come from you and you alone.</u>** *The Antagonists' Cookbook* is meant to design everyone else in your story.

Enjoy.

**RECIPES**

### Recipe #01 – Acromage Tahini

1 - #You can cast spells. Boost your Will attribute to superhuman capacity.

2 - Your acrobatic skills are beyond superhuman capacity and can replace your Speed attribute in certain situations (like fights).

3 - The second your firstborn draws breath, you'll stop aging and cannot die—until your last descendant dies. This could also apply to beings you create or "turn" (say, with a vampire's bite).

4 - You have hundreds of skills in your head (maybe more).

5 - You can heal from most injuries within a matter of seconds. Can you regrow lost body parts and shrug off zombie bites, too? Set the details.

### Recipe #02 – Adrenaline Bandit Wings

1 - #You're an athlete with peak human (maybe even superhuman) attributes.

2 - Whenever you're in a dangerous situation, you'll have unnaturally good luck—until the crisis ends. Then your luck returns to normal.

3 - Nothing scares you. Period.

4 - A certain number of times per day, you can pull off an improbable Speed-based feat. Something you'd normally fail at, even if you were a superhuman.

5 - #You are—or were—a professional villain. Pick up a criminal skill specialty that you can utilize, with superhuman capacity.

## Recipe #03 – Alchemical Parmesan

1 - #You're an alchemist with a finite number of potion formulas in your head. While they take time and materials to brew up, each potion's a temporary "power in a bottle.' Set the perks and limitations.

2 - You have a secret lab with the resources to pursue your field(s) of study.

3 - You can turn dead plant matter into devices and weapons (without changing the original look). Think "apple grenade" or "banana phone."

4 - Your skill with explosives is beyond superhuman capacity.

5 - You learn someone's weaknesses at a glance.

### Recipe #04 – Alien Vampire Flakes

1 - #You have enough alien blood in you to get the perks. Boost two of your attributes to superhuman capacity.

2 - #Whether you're a genius or just pretty quick-witted, you often make very good decisions—to the point where people tend to follow you.

3 - You can feed on the living, via touch. If your victim's a psychic, then you can hold onto that extra Health until it's removed by damage.

4 - You can trap your victims within their own minds. The comatose effect's indefinite and can't be undone by modern medicine. Feel free to merge another power(s) with this one.

5 - You can automatically sense the presence of psychic energies (and pinpoint the source) within a certain range.

### Recipe #05 – Almond Hunter-Killer

1 - #You're a well-versed killer. Your talents can be merely human or at superhuman capacity.

2 - You have an extensive network of reliable criminal contacts.

3 - Someone (or something) is obligated to watch your back. This could be a bodyguard, demon familiar, loyal AI, etc.

4 - You've got a focused beam attack that sucks life energy away from your target. Feel free to mix this effect with another power(s).

5 - You can turn living victims into inanimate objects.

### Recipe #06 – Android Spy Soup

1 - #You're some kind of robot. Boost three of your attributes to superhuman capacity.

2 - You have high-end sensors.

3 - You can teleport (with one passenger) across a certain range.

4 - You can move solid objects, either via telekinesis or some kind of tractor beam.

5 - #You are (or were) a spy, with a superhuman skill set.

### Recipe #07 – Aqua Alien Florentine

1 - #You have enough alien blood in you to get the perks. Boost two of your attributes to superhuman capacity.

2 - #You can turn into a living mass of liquid. If you wish this to be your permanent state, that's fine too.

3 - Stab someone and ice will pour from the wound (for a few seconds) as extra damage.

4 - You can maneuver and fight by sound alone.

5 - You've got some kind of edged attack that's a part of you (claws, horns, teeth, etc.).

### Recipe #08 – Aqua Gladiator Stroganoff

1 - #You can turn into a living mass of liquid. If you wish this to be your permanent state, that's fine too.

2 - You can create regular (or customized) archaic melee weapons out of thin air. Feel free to merge other powers with this one.

3 - You can shoot adhesive lines at a target (whether to climb or snare).

4 - During a fight, you'll be able to ignore your injuries (from broken bones to fatal wounds) until the fight's over—then it'll all catch up to you. Do note: certain injuries will still kill you on the spot (like decapitation or a nuke blast).

5 - Whenever fighting with a melee weapon in both hands, your attack feats are beyond superhuman capacity.

### Recipe #09 – Aquabeast Cheese Puffs

1 - You can turn into a part-human, part-animal hybrid (unless you prefer to be one full-time).

2 - Somehow, you can make liquids move (pretty much) however you want them to.

3 - This power allows you to talk to beasts and (usually) control them.

4 - Somehow, you can shoot a powerful stream(s) of water. How this works is up to you.

5 - #Whatever you are, you can't pass for a human. Boost two of your human-scale attributes to superhuman capacity. Set the details on what kind of creature you are.

### Recipe #10 – Archer's Curse Stir Fry

1 - #You are—or were—a professional villain. Pick up a criminal skill specialty that you can utilize, with superhuman capacity.

2 - When it comes to accuracy, your skill with the bow is beyond superhuman (even if you can't pause to aim).

3 - You've mastered a number of potent curse enchantments that can be inflicted upon your targets.

4 - Your costume and/or uniform counts as lightweight body armor.

5 - Your warning shots will automatically land where you want them to—but won't ever hurt anyone.

### Recipe #11 – Armor & Spinach Wrap

1 - You can make protective armor appear around you. Feel free to merge other powers into it.

2 - You have a focused beam attack that puts molten holes through most targets, with superhuman capacity.

3 - You can make entangling attacks upon your foes.

4 - #You're a well-versed killer. Your talents can be merely human or at superhuman capacity.

5 - #You're a cyborg, to the point where most of your body's been replaced with artificial components. Feel free to mix your other powers into this one. Are any of your attributes increased?

### Recipe #12 – Armor Sprouts

1 - #You can temporarily grow a bit taller and sprout extra muscles. Boost your Speed, Endurance, Might, and Health attributes to superhuman capacity. Set the details (including duration) and feel free to merge another power(s) with this one.

2 - You can make protective armor appear around you. Feel free to merge other powers into it.

3 - You can fly. Set the details and feel free to merge another power(s) with this one.

4 - Via teleportation, you can switch places with a target.

5 - You have hundreds of skills in your head (maybe more).

### Recipe #13 – Armored Fae Slaw

1 - #You can indefinitely shrink yourself. Work out the pros and cons of being smaller.

2 - #Whatever you are, you can't pass for a human. Boost two of your human-scale attributes to superhuman capacity. Set the details on what kind of creature you are.

3 - Your battle armor protects you from damage and raises your Might attribute to superhuman capacity. What other features does it have? Feel free to merge another power(s) with this one.

4 - #You can cast spells. Boost your Will attribute to superhuman capacity.

5 - You've got a secret lair, with sufficient resources to pursue your objectives (whatever they may be).

## Recipe #14 – Assembly Line Guacamole

1 - You have a secret lab with the resources to pursue your field(s) of study.

2 - You can create normal humans—without any powers.

3 - You have a useful, chatty object (like an implant, ship's AI, or talking mage's staff). Feel free to merge your other (relevant) powers with it.

4 - There's a serum that offers one random power, when ingested. Feel free to mix this one with another power(s).

5 - You have a knowledge of genetics that's beyond superhuman. With the right resources, think of the possibilities . . .

### Recipe #15 – Axe Killer Patties

1 - You have a nigh-indestructible melee weapon. In your hands, does it inflict normal or superhuman damage?

2 - You have a skill with axes that's beyond superhuman.

3 - During a fight, you'll be able to ignore your injuries (from broken bones to fatal wounds) until the fight's over—then it'll all catch up to you. Do note: certain injuries will still kill you on the spot (like decapitation or a nuke blast).

4 - You can hide or sneak about with a skill that's beyond superhuman. That makes you among the stealthiest bastards alive.

5 - You can deflect a variety of distance attacks (from thrown chairs to gunfire). Hopefully, you have the means to safely deflect these attacks.

### Recipe #16 – Bacon Spirit Slaver

1 - You can hold spirits within you and (try to) tap into their collective abilities, memories, and skills. Set the pros and cons for this scary power.

2 - You can summon spirits of the dead. Set the perks and drawbacks.

3 - #You're a world-class expert in the occult, with secrets worth killing for.

4 - You have a one-of-a-kind, non-mystical weapon. You can wield it with superhuman skill. Its material strength is beyond superhuman capacity. Set the other details.

5 - The souls of your victims end up your loyal slaves. Lay out the perks and limitations of this macabre ability.

### Recipe #17 – Baked Cyberkiller

1 - #You're a cyborg, to the point where most of your body's been replaced with artificial components. Feel free to mix your other powers into this one. Are any of your attributes increased?

2 - Your skin self-hardens (like armor) just before anything harmful can hit you.

3 - You have a secret lab with the resources to pursue your field(s) of study.

4 - You can create high-tech weapons out of thin air.

5 - You have easy access to a vast amount of previously stored information (what kind is up to you).

### Recipe #18 – Bang Bang Armor

1 - Your battle armor protects you from damage and raises your Might attribute to superhuman capacity. What other features does it have? Feel free to merge another power(s) with this one.

2 - You can unleash mundane energy orbs, that explode on impact.

3 - You can dodge almost any attack you see coming. It's the "undodgeable" attacks that you have to worry about (like tidal waves, a bullet to the back, an angry telekinetic, etc.).

4 - You have access to tracking bugs and the means to monitor them.

5 - Your weapons, implants, and/or gear have safeguards against theft, sabotage, tampering, disarmament, etc.

## Recipe #19 – Basil & Medicine Man

1 - You can hold spirits within you and (try to) tap into their collective abilities, memories, and skills. Set the pros and cons for this scary power.

2 - You know how to do exorcisms (whether by ritual magic, a mystical object, innate power, or some other way).

3 - #Your skills at wilderness combat, survival, and tracking are at superhuman capacity.

4 - #You're a world-class expert in the occult, with secrets worth killing for.

5 - #You're an anointed follower of a higher (or darker) power. Boost either your Will or Intellect to superhuman capacity. Needless to say, your prayers tend to get answered quickly (but in strange and mysterious ways).

### Recipe #20 – Beastie Fettuccine

1 - #Whatever you are, you can't pass for a human. Boost two of your human-scale attributes to superhuman capacity. Set the details on what kind of creature you are.

2 - You have an extensive network of reliable criminal contacts.

3 - You can emit a focused chemical attack, which temporarily paralyzes targets, yet allows them to feel pain.

4 - You (and only you) can turn intangible, to the point where only psychic energies, sonics, ultra-dense matter, magic, and other phased matter can touch you.

5 - #You are—or were—a professional villain. Pick up a criminal skill specialty that you can utilize, with superhuman capacity.

### Recipe #21 – Berry Glacial Nuke

1 - You have a unique, feature-loaded vehicle (from a spy car to a missile to a star cruiser).

2 - You can release a super-cold gas. Almost any solid it hits becomes as brittle as glass.

3 - Your weapons, implants, and/or gear have safeguards against theft, sabotage, tampering, disarmament, etc.

4 - You can freeze the surrounding temperatures, at superhuman capacity.

5 - You've got a weapon of mass destruction: something with an effect that's beyond superhuman. Does it have to be lethal? No. Just know that it's overwhelmingly powerful. Feel free to mix other power(s) with it, then set the details.

### Recipe #22 – Berserker & Onion

1 - #You can just "snap" and plow into fights with a merciless rage and (temporarily) boosted Intellect. Do any other attributes increase to superhuman capacity? Will you only attack enemies, while enraged?

2 - If injured in a melee attack, your attacker will suffer the exact same injury.

3 - While you do need to sleep, you'll never become exhausted from sustained physical or mental activity.

4 - Whenever you kill someone, temporarily boost two of your human-scale attributes to superhuman.

5 - Within minutes of being injured/sick, you'll simply recover. How's it work? Also, what won't this power cure?

## Recipe #23 – Bioslaughter Muffins

1 - #Whatever you are, you can't pass for a human. Boost two of your human-scale attributes to superhuman capacity. Set the details on what kind of creature you are.

2 - Whenever you want to hurt someone, you'll sprout three random (but useful) powers. None of them can be tech-based, psychic, or mystical—just organic. Once the fight's over, they'll go away.

3 - You can turn invisible to all forms of detection (the five senses, psychics, tech, and even magic). Set the details and limitations.

4 - As long as you're moving around, incoming attacks tend to miss you. This power works at superhuman capacity—even on attacks you don't see coming. Of course, some attacks can't be dodged.

5 - If stunned, you'll regain consciousness within seconds.

### Recipe #24 – Blackberry Sword Sleuth

1 - #You have a superhuman flair for finding people and solving mysteries—whether you're a spy, lawman, freelance sleuth, or someone's pet enforcer.

2 - Your skill with a sword's beyond superhuman.

3 - You can teleport (with one passenger) across a certain range.

4 - You have a weapon that resembles a harmless object (like a guitar blaster or sword cane).

5 - You're famous (in a good way), which can come in handy—if you play your cards right.

### Recipe #25 – Blended Eye Beamer

1 - #You're old, wise, and can move like a prime athlete.

2 - You have some kind of kinetic beam attack. No, it doesn't do heat or explosive damage. It just pokes a hole through whatever it can penetrate.

3 - You can make a distance attack that can hit multiple targets, either at once or in very rapid succession.

4 - You can leap up, down, and across great distances. Even if your arm strength's human, your kicking strength's superhuman.

5 - If you die, your body goes "BOOM." How severe is the blast?

### Recipe #26 – Blind Boss Mushroom

1 - #While permanently blind, your other senses are superhuman. Feel free to merge any relevant powers with this one.

2 - You have a weapon that resembles a harmless object (like a guitar blaster or sword cane).

3 - #Whether you're a genius or just pretty quick-witted, you often make very good decisions—to the point where people tend to follow you.

4 - #You've mastered a non-mystical fighting style, which allows you to fight with superhuman capacity.

5 - You have an extensive network of reliable criminal contacts.

## Recipe #27 – Bok Choy Grifter

1 - Don't kill anyone and no one will ever kill you. Period.

2 - #You are—or were—a professional villain. Pick up a criminal skill specialty that you can utilize, with superhuman capacity.

3 - Focus on a target and you'll instinctively guess three absolutely correct things about him/her/it.

4 - For some reason, moral individuals tend to like you (even your enemies).

5 - For some reason, evil beings tend to like you (even your enemies). That's why they're more likely to spare your life or attempt to recruit you (even against your will).

### Recipe #28 – Boss Armor Melon Bowl

1 - Your battle armor protects you from damage and raises your Might attribute to superhuman capacity. What other features does it have? Feel free to merge another power(s) with this one.

2 - Your overall Intellect attribute is at superhuman capacity.

3 - You can create a number of non-mystical barriers and forcefields, with flexibility on size and shape. How well do they protect against mystical attacks? Set the other details. Feel free to merge this ability with other powers.

4 - You have some kind of kinetic beam attack. No, it doesn't do heat or explosive damage. It just pokes a hole through whatever it can penetrate.

5 - You have a one-of-a-kind, non-mystical weapon. You can wield it with superhuman skill. Its material strength is beyond superhuman capacity. Set the other details.

### Recipe #29 – Boss Pad Thai

1 - #You can't feel emotions of any kind. Boost either your Intellect or Will attribute to superhuman capacity.

2 - Those trying to craft your doom will face multiple near-death experiences, per day, until they either stop or die trying.

3 - #Whether you're a genius or just pretty quick-witted, you often make very good decisions—to the point where people tend to follow you.

4 - #You've mastered a mystical fighting style. That's why your fighting and acrobatic abilities are at superhuman capacity, along with your striking damage.

5 - #You have accurate visions of the future. Set the details and limitations.

## Recipe #30 – Bound Djinn Sweet Roll

1 - #You're some kind of spectral entity (from a murdered soul to a possessive demon). Define your origins, strengths, and weaknesses.

2 - #You can cast spells. Boost your Will attribute to superhuman capacity.

3 - You have your very own pocket dimension. Assign the rules, perks, and drawbacks to such a place.

4 - Somehow, your innate powers were raised beyond superhuman levels. However, you also have a number of irritating weaknesses.

5 - #Somehow, information flows to you (from financial data to military secrets to occult mysteries to stuff no human should ever know). Set the details, origins, and any downsides.

### Recipe #31 – Brainwash Veal

1 - #You're a well-versed killer. Your talents can be merely human or at superhuman capacity.

2 - Establish some form of contact and you can alter a target's memories.

3 - You can create a number of non-mystical barriers and forcefields, with flexibility on size and shape. How well do they protect against mystical attacks? Set the other details. Feel free to merge this ability with other powers.

4 - Somehow, you can view a target (surroundings and all) from up to a certain range. Is this astral projection, magic, or something else? If relevant, you can mix this power with other abilities.

5 - Somehow, you can protect another being(s) from mental intrusions—from psychic shielding to serums to mind control spells. How's up to you.

### Recipe #32 – Brainwasher Sauté

1 - #You have enough telepathic DNA to read surface thoughts, at superhuman capacity. If desired, you can replace one of your other powers with something psychic.

2 - Establish some form of contact and you can alter a target's memories.

3 - You have a small arsenal of offensive and/or defensive gear.

4 - You can make a distance attack that can hit multiple targets, either at once or in very rapid succession.

5 - You can automatically sense the presence of psychic energies (and pinpoint the source) within a certain range.

### Recipe #33 – Bratwurst Mole Implant

1 - Your innate powers have a resistance to detection that's beyond superhuman. Thus, you can pass as "normal human" against sensors, psychics, and even magic.

2 - Your innate powers have a resistance to negation, theft, and manipulation that's beyond superhuman.

3 - Imagine you're facing a crisis and don't know how to get out of it. A number of non-mystical skills will enter your mind, in order to guide you through. Once things calm down, the skill(s) disappear.

4 - You have a resistance to torture that's beyond superhuman.

5 - If you die, your body goes "BOOM." How severe is the blast?

### Recipe #34 – Breaded Demon Spy

1 - #You've got demonic blood in you. Pick up one extra power and boost two of your attributes to superhuman. Now, what kind of demon are you?

2 - #You are (or were) a spy, with a superhuman skill set.

3 - You've got a mystical melee weapon that inflicts superhuman damage. Feel free to add any of your other powers to it.

4 - Only magic can harm you.

5 - You can change the moral alignment of others, at superhuman capacity.

## Recipe #35 – Broiled Mentor

1 - #Somehow, you're very wealthy (probably with billions to your name).

2 - Somehow, you can give someone a copy of your skill set(s).

3 - #You have extensive military experience and a natural affinity with any kind of weapon. Also, boost one of your attributes to superhuman capacity.

4 - #You have enough telepathic DNA to read surface thoughts, at superhuman capacity. If desired, you can replace one of your other powers with something psychic.

5 - #Whether you're a genius or just pretty quick-witted, you often make very good decisions—to the point where people tend to follow you.

## Recipe #36 – Broken Alignment Medley

1 - #You've mastered a mystical fighting style. That's why your fighting and acrobatic abilities are at superhuman capacity, along with your striking damage.

2 - Two of your attributes will become superhuman, whenever you fight foes of a different moral alignment.

3 - You can change the moral alignment of others, at superhuman capacity.

4 - You have (at least) one split personality.

5 - For better or worse, your name is feared far and wide. Set the pros and cons of having such an infamous rep.

### Recipe #37 – Brute Broth

1 - #Your Speed, Endurance, Might, and Health attributes are at the superhuman level. You can also self-regenerate by the minute.

2 - Whenever outnumbered in a fight, you (somehow) take way less damage than you should—even if fighting dozens-to-one. Why is this?

3 - If your strikes inflict any pain on a target, he/she/it will (somehow) lose consciousness.

4 - You can make a distance attack that can hit multiple targets, either at once or in very rapid succession.

5 - You're very adept at striking multiple targets, via melee attacks, practically at the same time. How does that work?

### Recipe #38 – Brutish Enchilada

1 - #Your Speed, Endurance, Might, and Health attributes are at the superhuman level. You can also self-regenerate by the minute.

2 - Only magic can harm you.

3 - Any clothing you wear has a superhuman toughness, until you take it off.

4 - You have access to a loyal group of combat-hardened minions. Give them gear and an origin story (hired mercs, temporary conjurations, members of your tribe, etc.).

5 - #You can't feel emotions of any kind. Boost either your Intellect or Will attribute to superhuman capacity.

## Recipe #39 – Caramel Volley

1 - If you attack a target (with a distance attack power, projectile, or thrown weapon), A number of copies will appear—just before impact—around the original. Are these copies temporary or permanent?

2 - With a touch, you can "program" an inanimate object to explode under a particular set of circumstances.

3 - You can throw non-weapon objects with a skill beyond superhuman. Whatever you can lift is fair game—from baseballs to lamps to crowded buses.

4 - You have access to high-end throwing weapons.

5 - You can make a distance attack that can hit multiple targets, either at once or in very rapid succession.

### Recipe #40 – Cat Burglar Deluxe

1  -  Your skill at bypassing security measures is beyond superhuman capacity.

2  -  You can stick to most surfaces and climb/walk/run/slither along them with ease.

3  -  You can turn invisible to all forms of detection (the five senses, psychics, tech, and even magic). Set the details and limitations.

4  -  Any target you strike (in melee combat) might forget the last few hours. Is this superhuman effect temporary or permanent?

5  -  As long as you're working/fighting alongside allies, your side will always beat the odds. Why?

### Recipe #41 – Chestnut Researcher

1 - #You have a superhuman flair for finding people and solving mysteries—whether you're a spy, lawman, freelance sleuth, or someone's pet enforcer.

2 - If you have the means to investigate (and a day's time), you can determine anyone's weakness(es).

3 - You have easy access to a vast amount of previously stored information (what kind is up to you).

4 - Touch an information-bearing object (books, flash drives, etc.) and you'll instantly know its content, with perfect recall.

5 - You have a perfect memory, capable of unlimited capacity.

## Recipe #42 – Chicken Ranch Figment

1 - You have the loyalty of a very dangerous being. Assign this individual three powers and a backstory.

2 - Aside from a handful of weaknesses, you're indestructible. Set the pros and cons of this power.

3 - When you wish, normal people can't sense you. The effect ends if you attack someone or if someone views you through a device. Anyone with a superhuman Will (or the right powers) can also spot you.

4 - You can sense the presence of threats and their general location(s).

5 - You can bring one fictional character into the real world at a time. Set the details. Feel free to merge other powers with this one.

### Recipe #43 – Child Sleuth Sardines

1 - #You're a remarkable kid. How is up to you. Pick one attribute and boost it to superhuman capacity.

2 - #You have a superhuman flair for finding people and solving mysteries—whether you're a spy, lawman, freelance sleuth, or someone's pet enforcer.

3 - Your skill at bypassing security measures is beyond superhuman capacity.

4 - You always find whatever you need to achieve your objective(s). Too bad having the right tools doesn't guarantee success.

5 - Until they see you in action, people tend to ignore and underestimate you.

### Recipe #44 – Chilled Pen Pal

1 - #You're a world-class expert in the occult, with secrets worth killing for.

2 - You've got some kind of special ink that'll force people to obey whatever instructions you write (with superhuman capacity).

3 - If you can get a piece of the target and create a likeness, whatever happens to your "doll" happens to the victim.

4 - You can reflect a mystical attack right back to its source—even if it's beyond superhuman capacity. Does this also apply to benign magicks?

5 - You have a useful network of mystical contacts.

### Recipe #45 – Cinnamon Stuck

1 - #You're a well-versed killer. Your talents can be merely human or at superhuman capacity.

2 - Merge this ability with any area-effect power/weapon you have. When using it, you can spare anyone or anything within its range (but nail everyone else). You just have to know where your "friendlies" are first, for this power to work.

3 - You can make a target(s) stick to a flat surface (like a wall, floor, or car door) with tons of force. Concentration's required.

4 - You have an extensive network of reliable criminal contacts.

5 - You know the precise location of every living thing around you.

### Recipe #46 – Coconut Witch Hunter

1 - #You're a well-versed killer. Your talents can be merely human or at superhuman capacity.

2 - Whenever outnumbered in a fight, you (somehow) take way less damage than you should—even if fighting dozens-to-one. Why is this?

3 - #You're an anointed follower of a higher (or darker) power. Boost either your Will or Intellect to superhuman capacity. Needless to say, your prayers tend to get answered quickly (but in strange and mysterious ways).

4 - You can automatically detect the presence of magic, within a certain range.

5 - You can reflect a mystical attack right back to its source—even if it's beyond superhuman capacity. Does this also apply to benign magicks?

## Recipe #47 – Combat Telekinetic Bread

1 - You can move solid objects, either via telekinesis or some kind of tractor beam.

2 - You can deflect a variety of distance attacks (from thrown chairs to gunfire). Hopefully, you have the means to safely deflect these attacks.

3 - When merged with this ability, certain powers (like telekinesis) can stay active for a while longer—even after an interruption of some kind (like lost concentration or contact). Hopefully, this will buy you enough time to re-establish the ability or beat a hasty retreat. Set the duration.

4 - If hit by a distance attack, you can instinctively retaliate—if you have the means to do so.

5 - You can clearly see through layers of inorganic matter without difficulty.

### Recipe #48 – Copycat Pancakes

1 - You can make temporary (and perfect) copies of any being you touch.

2 - You can create multiple, temporary copies of yourself.

3 - Touch an object and you can make a perfect copy of it.

4 - If you attack a target (with a distance attack power, projectile, or thrown weapon), A number of copies will appear—just before impact—around the original. Are these copies temporary or permanent?

5 - #You're a world-class expert in the occult, with secrets worth killing for.

### Recipe #49 – Corrupt Speedster Bites

1 - #You're a speedster, which allows you to move at superhuman capacity (possibly faster than sound).

2 - You're famous (in a good way), which can come in handy—if you play your cards right.

3 - You have a high-powered firearm of some kind, which does superhuman damage.

4 - #You have a superhuman flair for finding people and solving mysteries—whether you're a spy, lawman, freelance sleuth, or someone's pet enforcer.

5 - #You are—or were—a professional villain. Pick up a criminal skill specialty that you can utilize, with superhuman capacity.

### Recipe #50 – Creamy Super Spy

1  -  #You are (or were) a spy, with a superhuman skill set.

2  -  #You're cursed to stumble into constant dangers that you must never avoid (or you will suffer).

3  -  You automatically sense when other people (within a certain range) are in danger, including enough details to interfere—if you want to.

4  -  You have a small arsenal of offensive and/or defensive gear.

5  -  You always find whatever you need to achieve your objective(s). Too bad having the right tools doesn't guarantee success.

### Recipe #51 – Crisped Power Thief

1 - #You've mastered a non-mystical fighting style, which allows you to fight with superhuman capacity.

2 - You can steal innate powers.

3 - If fighting a foe with an ability that's beyond superhuman, pick one of your powers and raise it to match. When the fight ends, that spiked ability returns to superhuman capacity.

4 - You can "see" the innate powers of anyone (or anything) you look upon.

5 - You always make the first move (assuming you can move at all), whether in a fight or any other reflex-dependent event.

### Recipe #52 – Cryo Villain Chutney

1 - #You are—or were—a professional villain. Pick up a criminal skill specialty that you can utilize, with superhuman capacity.

2 - You can emit a beam that inflicts superhuman cold damage and encases whatever it hits in solid ice. Feel free to merge another power(s) with this one.

3 - You have a suit of durable, self-mending armor. Feel free to fold your other power(s) into it.

4 - In a sub-zero environment, your Speed, Endurance, Might, and Health attributes all become superhuman. Once removed from it, those attributes will return to normal.

5 - #You're a super genius with a number of non-violent skill masteries (set the details). Boost your Intellect to superhuman capacity.

### Recipe #53 – Cucumber Prankster

1 - You can create audio-visual holographic illusions.

2 - Your skill with disguises and impressions is beyond superhuman.

3 - You're invulnerable to illusions of any kind.

4 - Your voice can hypnotize targets, at superhuman capacity.

5 - #You have an overwhelming need to do good—even if you're a benign crook. Boost two of your attributes to superhuman capacity.

### Recipe #54 – Curried Luck Demigod

1 - #You have the blood of a deity running through your veins. Boost one of your human-scale attributes to superhuman capacity and one of your powers beyond superhuman.

2 - Whenever you're in a dangerous situation, you'll have unnaturally good luck—until the crisis ends. Then your luck returns to normal.

3 - #You are stunningly attractive and/or charismatic, which allows you to convince people to do what you want.

4 - Your skill at games of chance—and cheating at them—is beyond superhuman.

5 - You have unnaturally good luck—until you enter any kind of dangerous scenario. Then your luck's just typical.

### Recipe #55 – Curse Fist Soup

1 - #You've mastered a mystical fighting style. That's why your fighting and acrobatic abilities are at superhuman capacity, along with your striking damage.

2 - You can create regular (or customized) archaic distance weapons out of thin air. Feel free to merge other powers with this one.

3 - You've mastered a number of potent curse enchantments that can be inflicted upon your targets.

4 - If someone (or something) beats you up and leaves the area, half of your injuries will mend within a minute.

5 - #You're old, wise, and can move like a prime athlete.

### Recipe #56 – Cyber Stretch Pasta


1 - #You're a cyborg, to the point where most of your body's been replaced with artificial components. Feel free to mix your other powers into this one. Are any of your attributes increased?


2 - #You're playfully insane—until angered. Also, your mind's immune to mental intrusions of any kind. Boost your Endurance, Will, or Intellect to superhuman capacity.


3 - You can elongate your arms and legs.


4 - You can make protective armor appear around you. Feel free to merge other powers into it.


5 - You can induce madness within a target's mind (at superhuman capacity).

### Recipe #57 – Cyberwing Beef Bowl

1 - #You have extensive military experience and a natural affinity with any kind of weapon. Also, boost one of your attributes to superhuman capacity.

2 - You've got some kind of wings, which allow you to fly. Feel free to combine another power(s) into this one.

3 - #You're a cyborg, to the point where most of your body's been replaced with artificial components. Feel free to mix your other powers into this one. Are any of your attributes increased?

4 - You have a high-powered firearm of some kind, which does superhuman damage.

5 - You have access to a specialized projectile. If it wounds a target, it'll explode if removed or remote-detonated.

### Recipe #58 – Death Demigod Omelet

1 - #You have the blood of a deity running through your veins. Boost one of your human-scale attributes to superhuman capacity and one of your powers beyond superhuman.

2 - You own a very special mount with a mind of its own and one free power.

3 - If murdered, you can swap bodies with your killer.

4 - For some reason, evil beings tend to like you (even your enemies). That's why they're more likely to spare your life or attempt to recruit you (even against your will).

5 - #You can cast spells. Boost your Will attribute to superhuman capacity.

### Recipe #59 – Death's Minion Loaf

1 - #You're a powerful minion (with perks and flaws) who answers to Death. Pick up two extra powers that will help with your duties.

2 - If you wish, technological devices can't detect you—from cameras to high-end sensors.

3 - You can heal from most injuries within a few minutes.

4 - You never have to sleep.

5 - You can safely cross into other dimensions (with decent odds of safe return).

### Recipe #60 – Demon Brawler Blintz

1 - #You've got demonic blood in you. Pick up one extra power and boost two of your attributes to superhuman. Now, what kind of demon are you?

2 - You've got some kind of wings, which allow you to fly. Feel free to combine another power(s) into this one.

3 - Your voice can hypnotize targets, at superhuman capacity.

4 - You have an unarmed fighting skill that's beyond superhuman levels.

5 - You can unleash a mystical flame that inflicts superhuman damage.

### Recipe #61 – Demon Crooner Dip

1 - #You've got demonic blood in you. Pick up one extra power and boost two of your attributes to superhuman. Now, what kind of demon are you?

2 - You can feed on a target's life energy (and heal yourself), via song. Feel free to merge another power(s) with this one.

3 - Sing to an audience and you can read a number of minds at a time, with superhuman capacity.

4 - Establish some form of contact and you can alter a target's memories.

5 - You can manipulate a target's internal organs, blood flow, and overall health—whether to heal, torture, or even kill. If feasible, you can merge one/more abilities with this one.

### Recipe #62 – Demon Rider Licorice

1 - #You've got demonic blood in you. Pick up one extra power and boost two of your attributes to superhuman. Now, what kind of demon are you?

2 - If killed in the presence of mystical evil, you'll quickly self-resurrect.

3 - You own a very special mount with a mind of its own and one free power.

4 - You can unleash a mystical flame that burns both the flesh and any goodness within the soul. Anyone this power doesn't kill might end up corrupted by it.

5 - You can automatically track a number of targets anywhere on the globe.

## Recipe #63 – Deviled Stench

1 - You can alter your scent well enough to mimic someone else's, smell like a certain object(s), or even mask your smell.

2 - You have access to an incurable toxin. Feel free to merge another power(s) with this one.

3 - Somehow, you can make, obtain, or excrete potent but untraceable chemicals.

4 - You can undo the effect(s) of one of your other powers—unless you're too late.

5 - You can release pheromones, which bend the wills (and sex drives) of others.

### Recipe #64 – Devil's Advocate Salsa

1 - Bad things happen to those who break an agreement with you. Feel free to mix another power(s) with this one.

2 - #Somehow, you're very wealthy (probably with billions to your name).

3 - You've mastered a number of potent curse enchantments that can be inflicted upon your targets.

4 - You can safely cross into other dimensions (with decent odds of safe return).

5 - #You have a superhuman mastery of one non-mystical skill set (from doctor to pianist to CEO).

### Recipe #65 – Dipped Dragon Daddy

1 - #You're a full-blooded dragon. Aside from the wings, enhanced attributes, armored scales, and a breath attack, add the little perks and flaws.

2 - Any offspring you have will grow to full maturity within a matter of hours. Set the details on how this happens (alien DNA, magic, genetic flaw, etc.).

3 - #You are stunningly attractive and/or charismatic, which allows you to convince people to do what you want.

4 - #You can copy the appearance and voices of other humanoid beings.

5 - You can impregnate a living victim and expect one/more offspring within a number of hours. The rapid gestation will probably kill the host. Set the details on how this happened (sex, monster bite, mystical curse, viral sting, etc.).

### Recipe #66 – Drone Soufflé

1 - #You're some kind of robot. Boost three of your attributes to superhuman capacity.

2 - Some kind of concealable weaponry's been implanted within your body.

3 - You can turn parts of your body into small devices. Set the details and limitations. Feel free to merge another power(s) with this one.

4 - You have a useful, chatty object (like an implant, ship's AI, or talking mage's staff). Feel free to merge your other (relevant) powers with it.

5 - Any tech you make/own/use can (to a point) repair itself.

### Recipe #67 – Drunken Kielbasa

1 - #Each type (or even brand) of alcohol will give you a different, temporary power.

2 - #You're cursed to stumble into constant dangers that you must never avoid (or you will suffer).

3 - Somehow, you can make liquids move (pretty much) however you want them to.

4 - You can create non-mystical liquids out of thin air.

5 - You have an incredibly light, indestructible throwing weapon. Your skill with it is at superhuman capacity.

### Recipe #68 – Dutch Apple Hexter

1 - #You can enchant objects—both temporarily and permanently.

2 - One/more of your other powers can move through electronic devices (phones, radios, etc.) and affect someone on the other end.

3 - You answer to someone (or something) with a lot of useful connections and influence. This individual can ease your path, save your life, or have you killed for too many failures.

4 - In your hands, any mundane weapon inflicts its regular damage and/or superhuman mystical damage. The effect ends right after you let the weapon go.

5 - Any damage you sustain from mystical attacks is reduced to human capacity.

### Recipe #69 – Earth Elemental Tacos

1 - #You're a powerful minion who answers to Nature itself, via the element of earth. Pick up two extra powers that will help with your duties.

2 - Find enough natural ground and you can make it wrap around you (as a form-fitting armor), with three of your attributes boosted to superhuman levels.

3 - Anything you build or create can only be destroyed by magic. Feel free to merge any relevant power(s) with this one.

4 - #You've mastered a mystical fighting style. That's why your fighting and acrobatic abilities are at superhuman capacity, along with your striking damage.

5 - You can go without eating, drinking, resting, or even sleeping for days at a time.

### Recipe #70 – Earthquake Pudding

1 - You can start earthquakes and maintain them for as long as you concentrate.

2 - Stand on natural ground and you can erupt from another patch of ground—anywhere else in the world.

3 - You can make natural ground open or close at will. Feel free to merge another power(s) with this one.

4 - #You're a plant-based lifeform and cannot pass for human.

5 - You can automatically track a number of targets anywhere on the globe.

## Recipe #71 – Elemental Warrior Mousse

1 - #You have extensive military experience and a natural affinity with any kind of weapon. Also, boost one of your attributes to superhuman capacity.

2 - The proximity of natural ground allows you to regenerate (from most injuries) by the second.

3 - You can use water for scrying (spying) purposes.

4 - You can hover (or outright fly) on currents of air.

5 - You can control existing flames—but not generate them.

### Recipe #72 – Euphoria Sandwich

1 - You can release an area-effect field of temporary, paralytic bliss (which might be addictive to your targets).

2 - Merge this ability with any area-effect power/weapon you have. When using it, you can spare anyone or anything within its range (but nail everyone else). You just have to know where your "friendlies" are first, for this power to work.

3 - When merged with this ability, certain powers (like telekinesis) can stay active for a while longer—even after an interruption of some kind (like lost concentration or contact). Hopefully, this will buy you enough time to re-establish the ability or beat a hasty retreat. Set the duration.

4 - You can generate a vampiric energy burst, which will drink psychic energy from everyone in the blast radius—and convert it into extra Health. Set the details and limitations.

5 - You answer to someone (or something) with a lot of useful connections and influence. This individual can ease your path, save your life, or have you killed for too many failures.

### Recipe #73 – Executioner Pie

1 - Anyone you kill cannot come back from the dead or be revived.

2 - You've got a mystical distance weapon that inflicts superhuman damage. Feel free to merge any of your other powers with it.

3 - If you wish, your target won't be able to heal (or be healed) from weapon-based damage that you inflict. The effect lasts for days.

4 - You have a useful network of mystical contacts.

5 - #You're a well-versed killer. Your talents can be merely human or at superhuman capacity.

## Recipe #74 – Face-Lift Marinara

1 - Somehow, you can change a target's appearance, ethnicity, or even gender.

2 - You can make someone older, at a rate of years per touch.

3 - You can make someone younger, at a rate of years per touch.

4 - #You are (or were) a spy, with a superhuman skill set.

5 - You can manipulate a target's internal organs, blood flow, and overall health—whether to heal, torture, or even kill. If feasible, you can merge one/more abilities with this one.

### Recipe #75 – Fallen Elf Chips

1 - #You have enough elven blood to get the perks (attributes, skills, longevity, mystical advantages, etc.).

2 - #You're an anointed follower of a higher (or darker) power. Boost either your Will or Intellect to superhuman capacity. Needless to say, your prayers tend to get answered quickly (but in strange and mysterious ways).

3 - You can create regular (or customized) archaic distance weapons out of thin air. Feel free to merge other powers with this one.

4 - Do a kill and your victims' life energies will flow into you and instantly heal some/all of your injuries. Set the details.

5 - Whenever you're in danger, you'll pick up three offensive mystical powers. They'll be relevant to the crisis at hand, then go away when things calm down.

**Recipe #76 – Feta Spinach Acolyte**

    1 - #You're an anointed follower of a higher (or darker) power. Boost either your Will or Intellect to superhuman capacity. Needless to say, your prayers tend to get answered quickly (but in strange and mysterious ways).

    2 - You can summon spirits of the dead. Set the perks and drawbacks.

    3 - You can put your victim's soul into an object (like a weapon, amulet, or coin). Anyone it touches can tap into that soul's memories, skills, or powers—pick one and set the details.

    4 - Any clothing you wear has a superhuman toughness, until you take it off.

    5 - You can use a holy symbol(s) to repel creatures of an opposite morality.

## Recipe #77 – Fire Elemental Bologna

1 - #You're a powerful minion who answers to Nature itself, via the element of fire. Pick up two extra powers that will help with your duties.

2 - If immersed in flame, each of your innate powers will spike beyond superhuman levels. Hopefully, you're fireproof.

3 - You can increase the surrounding temperature to lethal levels.

4 - With superhuman capacity, you can make a target burst into flames.

5 - You're invulnerable to heat and fire—but is your gear?

**Recipe #78 – Fortune-Teller Sundae**

1 - #You have accurate visions of the future. Set the details and limitations.

2 - You can find a target anywhere in existence—even across dimensions.

3 - Somehow, you can view a target (surroundings and all) from up to a certain range. Is this astral projection, magic, or something else? If relevant, you can mix this power with other abilities.

4 - You can contact beings in other dimensions.

5 - Focus on a target and you'll instinctively guess three absolutely correct things about him/her/it.

## Recipe #79 – Fried Crystal Monster

1 - You can tunnel through solid surfaces.

2 - #You can turn into moving, living crystal. Boost two of your attributes to superhuman capacity. Set the details (including whether or not this is your natural state).

3 - You've got some kind of edged attack that's a part of you (claws, horns, teeth, etc.).

4 - You can regenerate by feeding on silicates (glass, sand, quartz, etc.).

5 - You can convert other beings into whatever you are (and pass along powers, skills, weaknesses, etc.). Anyone you train/turn is inclined to obey you.

### Recipe #80 – Frostbite Sorbet


1 - You can freeze the surrounding temperatures, at superhuman capacity.


2 - You're utterly immune to the cold.


3 - You can emit a beam that inflicts superhuman cold damage and encases whatever it hits in solid ice. Feel free to merge another power(s) with this one.


4 - For some reason, evil beings tend to like you (even your enemies). That's why they're more likely to spare your life or attempt to recruit you (even against your will).


5 - #Your skills at wilderness combat, survival, and tracking are at superhuman capacity.

### Recipe #81 – Frosted Memory Scholar

1 - With this power, you can establish a one-way mental contact and copy some/all of a target's memories to your own.

2 - When you die, any of your innate powers and mystical items will automatically go to a pre-designated heir(s).

3 - You have a perfect memory, capable of unlimited capacity.

4 - You have easy access to a vast amount of previously stored information (what kind is up to you).

5 - You have hundreds of skills in your head (maybe more).

### Recipe #82 – Glazed Enforcer

1 - #You are—or were—a professional villain. Pick up a criminal skill specialty that you can utilize, with superhuman capacity.

2 - You have a small arsenal of offensive and/or defensive gear.

3 - For better or worse, your name is feared far and wide. Set the pros and cons of having such an infamous rep.

4 - You can remotely hack into computers (via psychics, magic, or a bit of both).

5 - Your battle armor protects you from damage and raises your Might attribute to superhuman capacity. What other features does it have? Feel free to merge another power(s) with this one.

### Recipe #83 – Gluten Free Saboteur

1 - Your costume and/or uniform counts as lightweight body armor.

2 - Normally, it takes two actions to draw a weapon then use it. Well, you're so fast that you can make it count as one action. If feasible, this advantage can also be applied to another power(s).

3 - You have a high-powered firearm of some kind, which does superhuman damage.

4 - You can teleport (with one passenger) across a certain range.

5 - Complex devices just "happen" to break down in your proximity.

### Recipe #84 – Gooey Monster Fudge

1 - #Whatever you are, you can't pass for a human. Boost two of your human-scale attributes to superhuman capacity. Set the details on what kind of creature you are.

2 - Most physical impacts and projectiles harmlessly pass through you (like you're made of mud). Set the details, including which attacks can hurt you.

3 - You can heal from most injuries within a matter of seconds. Can you regrow lost body parts and shrug off zombie bites too?

4 - Somehow, you can spray a fast-acting corrosive. Set the details (range, potency, etc.).

5 - You can establish two-way, telepathic communications with anyone in your line of sight.

**Recipe #85 – Ground Starship**

1 - You have a unique, feature-loaded vehicle (from a spy car to a missile to a star cruiser).

2 - You have access to a portal designed for interstellar travel.

3 - You have access to a loyal group of combat-hardened minions. Give them gear and an origin story (hired mercs, temporary conjurations, members of your tribe, etc.).

4 - #You were born in a vastly different time period (past or future). Set the backstory.

5 - You have a useful, chatty object (like an implant, ship's AI, or talking mage's staff). Feel free to merge your other (relevant) powers with it.

## Recipe #86 – Hazelnut Psi-Pill Addict

1 - You have access to an addictive drug. Set the details and feel free to merge it with other powers.

2 - You can temporarily copy the innate psychic powers of those around you—as long as they stay within your power's range.

3 - Extend the duration of another power's effect(s), if feasible.

4 - If a mental attack gets through to your mind, this power will automatically repel the intrusion (a few times per day).

5 - You can automatically sense the presence of psychic energies (and pinpoint the source) within a certain range.

### Recipe #87 – Henchperson Noodles

1 - #Your Speed, Endurance, Might, and Health attributes are at the superhuman level. You can also self-regenerate by the minute.

2 - You can fly. Set the details and feel free to merge another power(s) with this one.

3 - You can teleport anywhere in the world.

4 - You answer to someone (or something) with a lot of useful connections and influence. This individual can ease your path, save your life, or have you killed for too many failures.

5 - Your skin's hardened against both physical and mundane energy attacks.

### Recipe #88 – Herbal Phasic Sumo

1 - #You're built like a sumo wrestler—with superhuman Might and Endurance.

2 - You can phase inanimate matter.

3 - You (and only you) can turn intangible, to the point where only psychic energies, sonics, ultra-dense matter, magic, and other phased matter can touch you.

4 - Complex devices just "happen" to break down in your proximity.

5 - #You are—or were—a professional villain. Pick up a criminal skill specialty that you can utilize, with superhuman capacity.

### Recipe #89 – Hive Kebab

1 - #You're part of a hive mind. Set the details. Feel free to merge another relevant power(s) with this one.

2 - You have an extensive network of reliable criminal contacts.

3 - #You're a well-versed killer. Your talents can be merely human or at superhuman capacity.

4 - You can convert other beings into whatever you are (and pass along powers, skills, weaknesses, etc.). Anyone you train/turn is inclined to obey you.

5 - You have hundreds of skills in your head (maybe more).

### Recipe #90 – Homestyle Death Blow

1 - #You've mastered a mystical fighting style. That's why your fighting and acrobatic abilities are at superhuman capacity, along with your striking damage.

2 - You can use another power on a target, yet delay its effect(s) for hours at a time.

3 - If you wish, the corpses of your victims will vanish without a trace. Feel free to merge one/more of your other abilities with this one.

4 - If engaged in a dangerous situation, you can temporarily absorb additional damage (well into the superhuman range). This "extra Health" goes away when the threat does, so be careful.

5 - A single blow to a living target (in armed or unarmed combat) should be considered a death blow. Even a punch to the jaw might count.

### Recipe #91 – Iceform Parfait

1 - #You can turn into a being of solid ice or cold energy (pick one). Set the details—including whether or not you want to permanently be this way.

2 - In a sub-zero environment, your Speed, Endurance, Might, and Health attributes all become superhuman. Once removed from it, those attributes will return to normal.

3 - In a sub-zero environment, your Intellect, Will, and Alertness attributes will increase to superhuman levels. Once removed from it, those attributes will return to normal.

4 - You can create regular (or customized) archaic melee weapons out of thin air. Feel free to merge other powers with this one.

5 - You can safely exist in most hazardous environments.

### Recipe #92 – Imposter Steak

1 - #You're a speedster, which allows you to move at superhuman capacity (possibly faster than sound).

2 - You always find whatever you need to achieve your objective(s). Too bad having the right tools doesn't guarantee success.

3 - You've got a personal forcefield that protects you from damage and can alter your appearance, via holographics (to a point).

4 - Your skill with disguises and impressions is beyond superhuman.

5 - #Whether you're a genius or just pretty quick-witted, you often make very good decisions—to the point where people tend to follow you.

### Recipe #93 – Imposter Waffles

1 - #You are—or were—a professional villain. Pick up a criminal skill specialty that you can utilize, with superhuman capacity.

2 - You can temporarily copy the innate organic (non-psychic) powers of those around you—as long as they stay within your power's range.

3 - #You can copy the appearance and voices of other humanoid beings.

4 - You can persuade folks to do things your way with superhuman capacity.

5 - Get close enough to a living target and you can copy his/hers/its skills.

### Recipe #94 – Instigator Bisque

1 - #You're some kind of spectral entity (from a murdered soul to a possessive demon). Define your origins, strengths, and weaknesses.

2 - This power can make your victims violently hate anyone/anything you wish, at superhuman capacity.

3 - The souls of your victims end up your loyal slaves. Lay out the perks and limitations of this macabre ability.

4 - You can rip a living being's soul loose and either hold on to it for a while—or let it go off into the afterlife.

5 - You can possess (and temporarily resurrect) the dead—with full access to their memories and abilities.

### Recipe #95 – Jalapeño Battle Nun

1 - #You're an anointed follower of a higher (or darker) power. Boost either your Will or Intellect to superhuman capacity. Needless to say, your prayers tend to get answered quickly (but in strange and mysterious ways).

2 - If people lie to you, they will automatically lose access to their innate powers. How long does the negation last?

3 - You can create short-ranged teleportation portals, through which you can spy/attack/flee/maneuver.

4 - #You're a well-versed killer. Your talents can be merely human or at superhuman capacity.

5 - You can contact beings in other dimensions.

### Recipe #96 – Jellied Atlantean Exile

1 - #You have enough alien blood in you to get the perks. Boost two of your attributes to superhuman capacity.

2 - You can maneuver and fight by sound alone.

3 - You can heal from most injuries within a matter of seconds. Can you regrow lost body parts and shrug off zombie bites too?

4 - You can breathe underwater and endure the depths of any ocean on Earth.

5 - #You have enough telepathic DNA to read surface thoughts, at superhuman capacity. If desired, you can replace one of your other powers with something psychic.

### Recipe #97 – Joke Yogurt

1 - This power will make people fanatically loyal to you, at superhuman capacity.

2 - Until they see you in action, people tend to ignore and underestimate you.

3 - Your jokes (no matter how bad) can make your victim(s) laugh—at superhuman capacity. Feel free to merge another power(s) with this one.

4 - You can mimic any sound you hear with superhuman capacity (from voices to a full symphony orchestra).

5 - You can reflect any psychic power or attack back to its point of origin. Is this power flexible enough to allow benign mental contact to get through?

## Recipe #98 – Jungle Lord Vampire & Cheese

1 - #You're a truly evil monster who must feed upon the living to survive. Boost two of your human-scale attributes to superhuman capacity.

2 - This power allows you to talk to beasts and (usually) control them.

3 - You can convert other beings into whatever you are (and pass along powers, skills, weaknesses, etc.). Anyone you train/turn is inclined to obey you.

4 - #Your skills at wilderness combat, survival, and tracking are at superhuman capacity.

5 - For better or worse, your name is feared far and wide. Set the pros and cons of having such an infamous rep.

### Recipe #99 – Kidnapper Tiramisu

1 - You can teleport beings to you, as long as they're within your range and not too large.

2 - You have access to a powder/liquid that renders most targets unconscious upon contact. Duration and after-effects are up to you.

3 - No matter how careless you are with your secret identity, no one can figure it out unless you intentionally reveal it.

4 - You can persuade folks to do things your way with superhuman capacity.

5 - #You are—or were—a professional villain. Pick up a criminal skill specialty that you can utilize, with superhuman capacity.

### Recipe #100 – Lemon Glyph Armor

1 - You can control your weapons, constructs, and/or gear from far away.

2 - Your battle armor protects you from damage and raises your Might attribute to superhuman capacity. What other features does it have? Feel free to merge another power(s) with this one.

3 - Whenever you're in danger, you'll pick up three temporary and defensive mystical powers. They'll be relevant to the crisis at hand, then go away when things calm down.

4 - You've got an indestructible (mystical) item/weapon that'll return to you from anywhere. When using it, any feats you make are in the superhuman range. Any powers you merge with it will go beyond superhuman capacity.

5 - Your weapons, implants, and/or gear have safeguards against theft, sabotage, tampering, disarmament, etc.

### Recipe #101 – Lettuce-Wrapped Cyberspeedster

1 - #You're a cyborg, to the point where most of your body's been replaced with artificial components. Feel free to mix your other powers into this one. Are any of your attributes increased?

2 - #You're a speedster, which allows you to move at superhuman capacity (possibly faster than sound).

3 - Your costume and/or uniform counts as lightweight body armor.

4 - You can do hundreds of small actions per second (from trigger pulls to punches to fast-building something). What are the limitations?

5 - You can make damaged devices self-repair.

**Recipe #102 – Lime Murder Diva**

1 - #You are stunningly attractive and/or charismatic, which allows you to convince people to do what you want.

2 - #You're a well-versed killer. Your talents can be merely human or at superhuman capacity.

3 - You always find whatever you need to achieve your objective(s). Too bad having the right tools doesn't guarantee success.

4 - For better or worse, your name is feared far and wide. Set the pros and cons of having such an infamous rep.

5 - If your strikes inflict any pain on a target, he/she/it will (somehow) lose consciousness.

### Recipe #103 – Low-Fat Bone Claw

1 - #You're a well-versed killer. Your talents can be merely human or at superhuman capacity.

2 - Whenever you make a melee-ranged strike, any armor or barrier in your way will briefly phase. Thus, you could stab someone through a suit of armor (like it wasn't there) and kill its wearer.

3 - You've got some kind of edged attack that's a part of you (claws, horns, teeth, etc.).

4 - You can heal from most injuries within a few minutes.

5 - You have a hardened skeleton, which is useful in a crash or a fistfight.

### Recipe #104 – Macaroni & Critter

1 - #Whatever you are, you can't pass for a human. Boost two of your human-scale attributes to superhuman capacity. Set the details on what kind of creature you are.

2 - Lose an appendage and it can move on its own and reattach with ease. If it's utterly destroyed, it won't regenerate.

3 - Drink blood and you'll regenerate by the minute.

4 - Your body will expel harmful substances (drugs, toxins, shrapnel, etc.) within a matter of seconds. Does it work on infectious bites?

5 - #You can turn into a powdery being of some kind (like sentient snow, carnivorous alien death spores, nanites, etc.). If you wish, this can be your permanent form.

## Recipe #105 – Mad Sender Skillet

1 - Through some kind of contact, you can teleport a target up to a certain range.

2 - You're famous (in a good way), which can come in handy—if you play your cards right.

3 - This power gives you a resistance to being moved—either by force or via powers. This level of protection's beyond superhuman capacity.

4 - #You're old, wise, and can move like a prime athlete.

5 - #You're playfully insane—until angered. Also, your mind's immune to mental intrusions of any kind. Boost your Endurance, Will, or Intellect to superhuman capacity.

### Recipe #106 – Magno Armor Pakora

1 - Your battle armor protects you from damage and raises your Might attribute to superhuman capacity. What other features does it have? Feel free to merge another power(s) with this one.

2 - Some kind of concealable weaponry's been implanted within your body.

3 - You can fly. Set the details and feel free to merge another power(s) with this one.

4 - You can generate magnetic energy fields and use them to move ferrous objects. Set the details. Feel free to merge this ability with other relevant powers.

5 - Your devices/vehicles/gadgets can run on multiple sources of energy.

### Recipe #107 – Manipulator Goulash

1 - #You can temporarily bring images of objects (but not living beings) to life.

2 - You can make beings experience illusions (across all five senses), at superhuman capacity.

3 - From miles out, you can establish two-way telepathic contact with a handful of minds. Feel free to merge this power with other relevant abilities.

4 - You can control your weapons, constructs, and/or gear from far away.

5 - You're almost immune to all of your other powers (should they ever be used on you or somehow misfire).

### Recipe #108 – Marinated Sentry

1 - Close your eyes and you'll be able to "see" in all directions at the same time. Naturally, you can function/fight/read better this way. Set the details for this power.

2 - #You've mastered a non-mystical fighting style, which allows you to fight with superhuman capacity.

3 - Win a fight and your injuries (if any) will instantly heal.

4 - You can automatically detect the presence of magic, within a certain range.

5 - In your hands, any mundane weapon inflicts its regular damage and/or superhuman mystical damage. The effect ends right after you let the weapon go.

### Recipe #109 – Mastermind Meringue Pie

1 - #Somehow, information flows to you (from financial data to military secrets to occult mysteries to stuff no human should ever know). Set the details, origins, and any downsides.

2 - Somehow, you have a mastery of every skill in existence. These skills can be at human or superhuman capacity (your call). How'd you get this power?

3 - You have easy access to a vast amount of previously stored information (what kind is up to you).

4 - #Somehow, you're very wealthy (probably with billions to your name).

5 - You have access to a loyal group of combat-hardened minions. Give them gear and an origin story (hired mercs, temporary conjurations, members of your tribe, etc.).

## Recipe #110 – Meatball Minion

1 - You can ricochet off solid objects (without harm). This is useful in combat or transportation. Set the details for this ability.

2 - You can create short-ranged teleportation portals, through which you can spy/attack/flee/maneuver.

3 - You have a small arsenal of offensive and/or defensive gear.

4 - Your skin self-hardens (like armor) just before anything harmful can hit you.

5 - Your acrobatic skills are beyond superhuman capacity and can replace your Speed attribute in certain situations (like fights).

### Recipe #111 – Melted Spirit Hustler

1 - You can persuade folks to do things your way with superhuman capacity.

2 - Bad things happen to those who break an agreement with you. Feel free to mix another power(s) with this one.

3 - You can track any spirits within your range.

4 - You can put your victim's soul into an object (like a weapon, amulet, or coin). Anyone it touches can tap into that soul's memories, skills, or powers—pick one and set the details.

5 - You can put someone's deceased soul into a different corpse (and resurrect it). Feel free to merge this power with other (relevant) abilities.

### Recipe #112 – Metal Burst & Olives


1 - #You can't feel emotions of any kind. Boost either your Intellect or Will attribute to superhuman capacity.

2 - You can safely release a 360-degree shockwave.

3 - #You can turn into a metallic powerhouse, with your Might and Endurance attributes at superhuman capacity.

4 - Your distance attacks will pass through any type of energy-based barrier, as if it wasn't there. Any movement powers you might have (like teleportation) might pass through too.

5 - For better or worse, your name is feared far and wide. Set the pros and cons of having such an infamous rep.

### Recipe #113 – Metal Spinner Salmon

1 - #You can turn into a metallic powerhouse, with your Might and Endurance attributes at superhuman capacity.

2 - You can spin inhumanly fast, allowing you to travel over surfaces at a high rate of speed and inflict superhuman damage.

3 - You have an unarmed fighting skill that's beyond superhuman levels.

4 - #You're a genetic superhuman (born or augmented) with one free power and one superhuman attribute.

5 - #You're a super genius with a number of non-violent skill masteries (set the details). Boost your Intellect to superhuman capacity.

### Recipe #114 – Minced Multi-Gunner

1 - #You are—or were—a professional villain. Pick up a criminal skill specialty that you can utilize, with superhuman capacity.

2 - You have a one-of-a-kind, non-mystical weapon. You can wield it with superhuman skill. Its material strength is beyond superhuman capacity. Set the other details.

3 - You have some kind of variable-yield ammo (or possibly a power), which allows you to inflict different types of damage on a target. Examples would be gadget arrows, specialized bullets, or even assorted eye beams.

4 - You've got a secret lair, with sufficient resources to pursue your objectives (whatever they may be).

5 - #You're a genetic superhuman (born or augmented) with one free power and one superhuman attribute.

## Recipe #115 – Mindjacker Teriyaki

1 - You can indefinitely switch the minds of other beings (all at once), at superhuman capacity.

2 - Your mind has some kind of defense against psychic attacks, which functions at superhuman capacity.

3 - You can establish two-way psychic contact with up to hundreds of minds (maybe more), within a one-mile range.

4 - #You're meaner than most people. Boost your Endurance and Will attributes to superhuman levels.

5 - You can inflict total and permanent memory loss, with superhuman capacity. If you're feeling nice, you can pull your punches—but why?

### Recipe #116 – Mint Combat Alien

1 - #You have enough alien blood in you to get the perks. Boost two of your attributes to superhuman capacity.

2 - You have a noticeable organic armor that's permanently bonded to you (like a shell).

3 - You can heal from most injuries within a few minutes.

4 - You have a small arsenal of offensive and/or defensive gear.

5 - #You have extensive military experience and a natural affinity with any kind of weapon. Also, boost one of your attributes to superhuman capacity.

### Recipe #117 – Miso-Cured Sniper

1 - #Your skills at wilderness combat, survival, and tracking are at superhuman capacity.

2 - You have a high-powered firearm of some kind, which does superhuman damage.

3 - You have the loyalty of a very dangerous being. Assign this individual three powers and a backstory.

4 - If you selfishly retreat from a threat (without regard for anyone else), you'll always escape.

5 - Your sniper skills are beyond superhuman.

### Recipe #118 – Mixed Alchemical Gadgeteer

    1 - #You're an alchemist with a finite number of potion formulas in your head. While they take time and materials to brew up, each potion's a temporary "power in a bottle." Set the perks and limitations.

    2 - You have a small arsenal of offensive and/or defensive gear.

    3 - #With a touch, you can turn an inanimate object into something else. Set the limitations for this power.

    4 - #You are (or were) a spy, with a superhuman skill set.

    5 - You answer to someone (or something) with a lot of useful connections and influence. This individual can ease your path, save your life, or have you killed for too many failures.

### Recipe #119 – Mutagenic Slices

1 - You can make vegetation grow out of any solid surface (even without seeds).

2 - There's a serum that offers one random power, when ingested. Feel free to mix this one with another power(s).

3 - Somehow, you can make, obtain, or excrete potent but untraceable chemicals.

4 - You have a knowledge of genetics that's beyond superhuman. With the right resources, think of the possibilities . . .

5 - #You've got demonic blood in you. Pick up one extra power and boost two of your attributes to superhuman. Now, what kind of demon are you?

### Recipe #120 – Mystic Badge Frittata

1 - #By day, you're one person. By night, you (literally) morph into someone else. So yeah, generate another character (perhaps even someone without powers).

2 - When you die, any of your innate powers and mystical items will automatically go to a pre-designated heir(s).

3 - Your mind has some kind of defense against psychic attacks, which functions at superhuman capacity.

4 - You've got an indestructible (mystical) item/weapon that'll return to you from anywhere. When using it, any feats you make are in the superhuman range. Any powers you merge with it will go beyond superhuman capacity.

5 - #You have a superhuman flair for finding people and solving mysteries—whether you're a spy, lawman, freelance sleuth, or someone's pet enforcer.

### Recipe #121 – Mystic Gunsmith Pops

1 - Normally, it takes two actions to draw a weapon then use it. Well, you're so fast that you can make it count as one action. If feasible, this advantage can also be applied to another power(s).

2 - You can make long-distance attacks, at targets you can't directly see, with a skill that's beyond superhuman capacity.

3 - You can create man-portable, modern-day weaponry out of thin air. Feel free to merge another power(s) with this one.

4 - Your distance attacks will harmlessly pass through the first solid object they hit (like a wall or body armor), then turn solid again.

5 - Your distance attack(s) might miss a target but will never hit an innocent bystander or ally.

## Recipe #122 – Oats & Shock Villain

1 - You can power most devices, via physical contact.

2 - Every few seconds, you can dish out a radius-effect pulse that shuts down devices temporarily or permanently (choose now).

3 - You can draw Health from a mechanical power source, via touch, if you're sick or injured.

4 - You can release focused electrical bolts from great distances.

5 - Pick one of your other powers and permanently amplify it beyond superhuman capacity.

### Recipe #123 – Open-Faced Sand Dragon

1 - #You're a full-blooded dragon. Aside from the wings, enhanced attributes, armored scales, and a breath attack, add the little perks and flaws.

2 - #You can turn into a powdery being of some kind (like sentient snow, carnivorous alien death spores, nanites, etc.). If you wish, this can be your permanent form.

3 - You can phase beings into yourself and lock them into a sort of stasis. During this time, you can access their powers, attributes, and memories. Set the limitations for this ability.

4 - You can release an area-effect field of fear, at superhuman capacity.

5 - Think of your tongue as a ranged weapon. The range, damage types (barbed, acidic, whip, etc.), and other details are up to you.

### Recipe #124 – Oven-Fresh Dwarf Rage

1 - #You have enough dwarven blood to get the perks/limitations. What are they?

2 - You have a nigh-indestructible melee weapon. In your hands, does it inflict normal or superhuman damage?

3 - During a fight, you'll be able to ignore your injuries (from broken bones to fatal wounds) until the fight's over—then it'll all catch up to you. Do note: certain injuries will still kill you on the spot (like decapitation or a nuke blast).

4 - The presence of rage (either yours or someone else's) will temporarily boost your human-level attributes to superhuman capacity.

5 - Whenever outnumbered in a fight, you (somehow) take way less damage than you should—even if fighting dozens-to-one. Why is this?

### Recipe #125 – Pack Smoothie

1 - #You're a lycanthrope, with the appropriate perks and limitations. Pick a sub-breed (werewolf, weretiger, werebat, etc.).

2 - When you wish, normal people can't sense you. The effect ends if you attack someone or if someone views you through a device. Anyone with a superhuman Will (or the right powers) can also spot you.

3 - #You have a superhuman flair for finding people and solving mysteries—whether you're a spy, lawman, freelance sleuth, or someone's pet enforcer.

4 - You can create multiple, temporary copies of yourself.

5 - Your body will expel harmful substances (drugs, toxins, shrapnel, etc.) within a matter of seconds. Does it work on infectious bites?

## Recipe #126 – Peaches & Water Elemental

1 - #You're a powerful minion who answers to Nature itself, via the element of water. Pick two free water-based powers.

2 - Immersion in water boosts your Speed, Endurance, Might, and Health attributes—until you've been out of it for a while.

3 - If you immerse yourself in water, you can teleport to a watery location that's closest to your intended destination (like an ocean, pond, swimming pool, or even a filled bathtub). However far you can go, you'll always end up wet.

4 - If injured, you can regain Health by consuming safe liquids.

5 - #You can turn into a living mass of liquid. If you wish this to be your permanent state, that's fine too.

### Recipe #127 – Peanut Butter Portal Key

1 - You have your very own pocket dimension. Assign the rules, perks, and drawbacks to such a place.

2 - You've got an indestructible (mystical) item/weapon that'll return to you from anywhere. When using it, any feats you make are in the superhuman range. Any powers you merge with it will go beyond superhuman capacity.

3 - Stomp on a flat surface and some kind of barrier wall will shoot out of it (like stone, solid energy, etc.).

4 - You have access to a loyal group of combat-hardened minions. Give them gear and an origin story (hired mercs, temporary conjurations, members of your tribe, etc.).

5 - Your weapons, implants, and/or gear have safeguards against theft, sabotage, tampering, disarmament, etc.

### Recipe #128 – Peanut Plant Monster

1 - #You're a plant-based lifeform and cannot pass for human.

2 - You have extra arms. Are they retractable?

3 - #You can temporarily grow a bit taller and sprout extra muscles. Boost your Speed, Endurance, Might, and Health attributes to superhuman capacity. Set the details (including duration) and feel free to merge another power(s) with this one.

4 - You can impregnate a living victim and expect one/more offspring within a number of hours. The rapid gestation will probably kill the host. Set the details on how this happened (sex, monster bite, mystical curse, viral sting, etc.).

5 - You're immune to non-mystical toxins.

### Recipe #129 – Peas & Cursed Amulet

1 - You can use a holy symbol(s) to repel creatures of an opposite morality.

2 - You've mastered a number of potent curse enchantments that can be inflicted upon your targets.

3 - You've got an indestructible (mystical) item/weapon that'll return to you from anywhere. When using it, any feats you make are in the superhuman range. Any powers you merge with it will go beyond superhuman capacity.

4 - If you fail to notice something, you'll (somehow) spot it anyway—for a number of times per day. Note: this only works on threats you could possibly spot. The rest will still blindside you.

5 - You can make a sacrificial offering to a higher being, in exchange for whatever you want. The bigger the "ask," the bigger your offering has to be—from favors to wealth to victims. Set the details. Feel free to merge another power(s) with this one.

### Recipe #130 – Pecan Cyber Spy

1 - #You are (or were) a spy, with a superhuman skill set.

2 - #You are—or were—a professional villain. Pick up a criminal skill specialty that you can utilize, with superhuman capacity.

3 - You have access to a loyal group of combat-hardened minions. Give them gear and an origin story (hired mercs, temporary conjurations, members of your tribe, etc.).

4 - #You're a cyborg, to the point where most of your body's been replaced with artificial components. Feel free to mix your other powers into this one. Are any of your attributes increased?

5 - #Somehow, you're very wealthy (probably with billions to your name).

## Recipe #131 – Petrification Sausage

1 - #You can copy the appearance and voices of other humanoid beings.

2 - Somehow, you can turn a flesh-and-blood victim into inanimate matter.

3 - #Whatever you are, you can't pass for a human. Boost two of your human-scale attributes to superhuman capacity. Set the details on what kind of creature you are.

4 - You have extra heads attached to you—each with its own brain and independent personality.

5 - #While you may take damage normally, only a handful of things can truly kill you. Boost your Will, Endurance, or Health attribute to superhuman capacity.

### Recipe #132 – Phantom Comedian Primavera

1 - #You're some kind of spectral entity (from a murdered soul to a possessive demon). Define your origins, strengths, and weaknesses.

2 - Your jokes (no matter how bad) can make your victim(s) laugh—at superhuman capacity. Feel free to merge another power(s) with this one.

3 - You can turn living beings into zombies. Also, feel free to mix this ability with another power(s).

4 - If you wish, the corpses of your victims will vanish without a trace. Feel free to merge one/more of your other abilities with this one.

5 - You can indefinitely alter a target's entire worldview, with superhuman capacity.

### Recipe #133 – Phantom Dragon Mix

1 - #You're a full-blooded dragon. Aside from the wings, enhanced attributes, armored scales, and a breath attack, add the little perks and flaws.

2 - From miles out, you can establish two-way telepathic contact with a handful of minds. Feel free to merge this power with other relevant abilities.

3 - You are fireproof, to the point where flames will heal your injuries.

4 - When used against you, the power of mystical objects is reduced to human scale.

5 - You can turn invisible to all forms of detection (the five senses, psychics, tech, and even magic). Set the details and limitations.

### Recipe #134 – Pheromonal Salami

1 - #You are—or were—a professional villain. Pick up a criminal skill specialty that you can utilize, with superhuman capacity.

2 - You can release pheromones, which bend the wills (and sex drives) of others.

3 - Extend the duration of another power's effect(s), if feasible.

4 - You have an extensive network of reliable criminal contacts.

5 - You can induce madness within a target's mind (at superhuman capacity).

### Recipe #135 – Pickled Doomsday Lair

1 - You've got a secret lair, with sufficient resources to pursue your objectives (whatever they may be).

2 - You have access to a loyal group of combat-hardened minions. Give them gear and an origin story (hired mercs, temporary conjurations, members of your tribe, etc.).

3 - You've got a weapon of mass destruction: something with an effect that's beyond superhuman. Does it have to be lethal? No. Just know that it's overwhelmingly powerful. Feel free to mix other power(s) with it, then set the details.

4 - This power will make people fanatically loyal to you, at superhuman capacity.

5 - Pick another ability and multiply its range or count (but not duration) to your advantage.

### Recipe #136 – Plant Freak Cheese

1 - You can turn people, animals, or plants into different kinds of plant-based lifeforms—some of them carnivorous.

2 - You can shoot razor-sharp shards. What one material are they made of? Feel free to mix this power with any others you might have.

3 - #You're a plant-based lifeform and cannot pass for human.

4 - From miles out, you can establish two-way telepathic contact with a handful of minds. Feel free to merge this power with other relevant abilities.

5 - #Whether you're a genius or just pretty quick-witted, you often make very good decisions—to the point where people tend to follow you.

### Recipe #137 – Plant Monster S'mores

1 - #You're a plant-based lifeform and cannot pass for human.

2 - If attacked by a mental power, you can temporarily copy it (assuming you survive). Set the other details, like how many powers can you safely contain?

3 - If attacked by an organic (non-psychic) power, you can temporarily copy it (assuming you survive). Set the other details, like how many powers can you safely contain?

4 - You can convert other beings into whatever you are (and pass along powers, skills, weaknesses, etc.). Anyone you train/turn is inclined to obey you.

5 - You can unleash a lethal plague. How does it work? Don't be afraid to mix it in with your other powers. Lastly, does it affect you?

### Recipe #138 – Poached Witch Sniper

1 - #You can cast spells. Boost your Will attribute to superhuman capacity.

2 - You have a high-powered firearm of some kind, which does superhuman damage.

3 - Unless your shot is (somehow) ruined, you'll never miss a stationary target.

4 - Focus on a target and you'll instinctively guess three absolutely correct things about him/her/it.

5 - You can find a target anywhere in existence— even across dimensions.

### Recipe #139 – Power Thief Pancetta

1 - You can steal innate powers.

2 - You can control a living target's body, like one would a puppet.

3 - Somehow, you can view a target (surroundings and all) from up to a certain range. Is this astral projection, magic, or something else? If relevant, you can mix this power with other abilities.

4 - Get close enough to a living target and you can copy his/hers/its skills.

5 - #You have enough telepathic DNA to read surface thoughts, at superhuman capacity. If desired, you can replace one of your other powers with something psychic.

### Recipe #140 – Protean Crisp

    1 - #You have some kind of symbiote within your body (biological, psychic, tech-based, mystical, etc.). Feel free to merge your other power(s) with it.

    2 - You're an expert in almost everything alien, with a skill level that's beyond superhuman.

    3 - #With a touch, you can turn an inanimate object into something else. Set the limitations for this power.

    4 - You know the specifics of any ambush, just before it hits you.

    5 - You have an extensive network of extraterrestrial contacts.

### Recipe #141 – Psi-Rocker Brisket

1 - You can touch an object, charge it with psychic energy, then make it explode on impact.

2 - You can create temporary, simple, non-weapon objects of pure psychic energy. Set the details. Feel free to merge this ability with other (relevant) powers.

3 - You can create audio-visual holographic illusions.

4 - #You're a versatile musician-songwriter with a skill that's beyond superhuman.

5 - Your music can hypnotize live audiences, with superhuman capacity. Feel free to merge another power(s) with this one.

### Recipe #142 – Psi-Teacher Piperade

1 - #You have some kind of symbiote within your body (biological, psychic, tech-based, mystical, etc.). Feel free to merge your other power(s) with it.

2 - Somehow, you can give someone a copy of your skill set(s).

3 - Your overall Intellect attribute is at superhuman capacity.

4 - You have hundreds of skills in your head (maybe more).

5 - You can reflect any psychic power or attack back to its point of origin. Is this power flexible enough to allow benign mental contact to get through?

### Recipe #143 – Pureed Blood Sword

1 - Your weapons, implants, and/or gear have safeguards against theft, sabotage, tampering, disarmament, etc.

2 - #You're a predatory creature with unique dietary needs—but also some good left in you. Boost your Will and two other attributes to superhuman capacity.

3 - You can steal Health from anyone you touch—either to heal or just for the rush.

4 - You've got an indestructible (mystical) item/weapon that'll return to you from anywhere. When using it, any feats you make are in the superhuman range. Any powers you merge with it will go beyond superhuman capacity.

5 - You can convert other beings into whatever you are (and pass along powers, skills, weaknesses, etc.). Anyone you train/turn is inclined to obey you.

### Recipe #144 – Raspberry Psi-Vamp

1 - You can possess the living.

2 - With this power, you can establish a one-way mental contact and copy some/all of a target's memories to your own.

3 - If you can establish psychic contact, this power will let you feed on a target's mind without having to be in the room. Whether it's for sustenance, to recover lost Health, or both is up to you.

4 - You can indefinitely alter a target's entire worldview, with superhuman capacity.

5 - During a crisis, you'll sprout three random, useful, and defensive psychic abilities.

## Recipe #145 – Retired Swordsman Squash

1 - #You're old, wise, and can move like a prime athlete.

2 - You have a nigh-indestructible melee weapon. In your hands, does it inflict normal or superhuman damage?

3 - Your skill with a sword's beyond superhuman.

4 - Your skill with thrown weapons is beyond superhuman.

5 - A single blow to a living target (in armed or unarmed combat) should be considered a death blow. Even a punch to the jaw might count.

## Recipe #146 – Rigatoni Support Minion

1 - You can remotely hack into computers (via psychics, magic, or a bit of both).

2 - You have a small arsenal of offensive and/or defensive gear.

3 - You have a secret lab with the resources to pursue your field(s) of study.

4 - Your costume and/or uniform counts as lightweight body armor.

5 - #You have extensive military experience and a natural affinity with any kind of weapon. Also, boost one of your attributes to superhuman capacity.

### Recipe #147 – Roasted Bladeshielder

1 - #You have extensive military experience and a natural affinity with any kind of weapon. Also, boost one of your attributes to superhuman capacity.

2 - You have a form-fitting mundane forcefield, which offers you protection beyond superhuman capacity. Feel free to merge this power with other (relevant) ones.

3 - You have an energy-based melee weapon (like a flame sword or a plasma spear).

4 - Somehow, you can parry attacks with a skill that's beyond superhuman. While you could parry machine gun fire or a volley of arrows, can you do it safely?

5 - #You can temporarily grow a bit taller and sprout extra muscles. Boost your Speed, Endurance, Might, and Health attributes to superhuman capacity. Set the details (including duration) and feel free to merge another power(s) with this one.

### Recipe #148 – Rogue Apprentice Granola

1 - #You can cast spells. Boost your Will attribute to superhuman capacity.

2 - You answer to someone (or something) with a lot of useful connections and influence. This individual can ease your path, save your life, or have you killed for too many failures.

3 - Any clothing you wear has a superhuman toughness, until you take it off.

4 - You have a mystical object that can boost one of your other powers beyond superhuman capacity.

5 - Any damage you sustain from mystical attacks is reduced to human capacity.

### Recipe #149 – Saboteur Liverwurst

1 - #You are—or were—a professional villain. Pick up a criminal skill specialty that you can utilize, with superhuman capacity.

2 - You can sense an imminent danger (but not the details) before it happens.

3 - You can track any object you've ever sensed—as long as it's within your range.

4 - You can teleport small objects to you, as long as they're within your power's range.

5 - Your skills as an escape artist are beyond superhuman. With a skill this high, you can escape from Hell itself, much less any mortal prison.

## Recipe #150 – Sacrificial Weapons Plum

1 - You have access to a reliable network of allies within business, government, and other legitimate sectors of society. Set the details.

2 - You can make a sacrificial offering to a higher being, in exchange for whatever you want. The bigger the "ask," the bigger your offering has to be—from favors to wealth to victims. Set the details. Feel free to merge another power(s) with this one.

3 - You can create man-portable, modern-day weaponry out of thin air. Feel free to merge another power(s) with this one.

4 - No matter how careless you are with your secret identity, no one can figure it out unless you intentionally reveal it.

5 - #Somehow, you're very wealthy (probably with billions to your name).

### Recipe #151 – Saucy Vampire

1 - The more of a victim's blood you drink, the more memories you'll be able to access.

2 - #You're a truly evil monster who must feed upon the living to survive. Boost two of your human-scale attributes to superhuman capacity.

3 - You know the precise location of every living thing around you.

4 - You have a painful, paralytic bite.

5 - You can convert other beings into whatever you are (and pass along powers, skills, weaknesses, etc.). Anyone you train/turn is inclined to obey you.

### Recipe #152 – Sesame Armorer

1 - #You have the blood of a deity running through your veins. Boost one of your human-scale attributes to superhuman capacity and one of your powers beyond superhuman.

2 - Your skill with a sword's beyond superhuman.

3 - #Whether you're a genius or just pretty quick-witted, you often make very good decisions—to the point where people tend to follow you.

4 - You can generate magnetic energy fields and use them to move ferrous objects. Set the details. Feel free to merge this ability with other relevant powers.

5 - Your skills at building and carpentry are beyond superhuman.

### Recipe #153 – Shadow Broker Chili

1 - #You're a truly evil monster who must feed upon the living to survive. Boost two of your human-scale attributes to superhuman capacity.

2 - You can teleport from one shadow to another shadow, near your desired destination. Is this a super power or something mystical?

3 - #Somehow, information flows to you (from financial data to military secrets to occult mysteries to stuff no human should ever know). Set the details, origins, and any downsides.

4 - You can create short-ranged teleportation portals, through which you can spy/attack/flee/maneuver.

5 - You can feed on the living, via touch. If your victim's a mystical being, then you can hold onto that extra Health until it's removed by damage.

### Recipe #154 – Shield Sauce

1 - #You've mastered a non-mystical fighting style, which allows you to fight with superhuman capacity.

2 - You can deflect a variety of distance attacks (from thrown chairs to gunfire). Hopefully, you have the means to safely deflect these attacks.

3 - You have a one-of-a-kind, non-mystical weapon. You can wield it with superhuman skill. Its material strength is beyond superhuman capacity. Set the other details.

4 - You have a high-powered firearm of some kind, which does superhuman damage.

5 - You have a unique, feature-loaded vehicle (from a spy car to a missile to a star cruiser).

### Recipe #155 – Shock Casserole

1 - #You can turn into solid energy (pick one type). If feasible, feel free to merge another power(s) into this one.

2 - You can fly. Set the details and feel free to merge another power(s) with this one.

3 - You can release focused electrical bolts from great distances.

4 - Certain places (oceans, battlefields, forests, etc.) actually boost your powers beyond superhuman, as long as you're physically present. Once you leave, the effect fades (set the details).

5 - You can make a distance attack that can hit multiple targets, either at once or in very rapid succession.

### Recipe #156 – Shock Trooper Rice

1 - Your touch can inflict shock damage.

2 - #You have extensive military experience and a natural affinity with any kind of weapon. Also, boost one of your attributes to superhuman capacity.

3 - #You're a speedster, which allows you to move at superhuman capacity (possibly faster than sound).

4 - You have a form-fitting field of solid air that's invisible to the naked eye and protects you from most attacks.

5 - If under open sky, you can call down lightning upon your target(s).

### Recipe #157 – Singed Pyrokinetic

1 - You can control existing flames—but not generate them.

2 - #You can turn into a being of solid, moving, fire. Set up the perks and flaws of this ability.

3 - You can teleport (with one passenger) across a certain range.

4 - You can fly. Set the details and feel free to merge another power(s) with this one.

5 - If immersed in flames, your Speed, Endurance, Will, and Health attributes will become superhuman. Hopefully, you're fireproof.

### Recipe #158 – Smoky Pact Killer

1 - Bad things happen to those who break an agreement with you. Feel free to mix another power(s) with this one.

2 - #You're a well-versed killer. Your talents can be merely human or at superhuman capacity.

3 - Do a kill and your victims' life energies will flow into you and instantly heal some/all of your injuries.

4 - You have a one-of-a-kind, non-mystical weapon. You can wield it with superhuman skill. Its material strength is beyond superhuman capacity. Set the other details.

5 - The souls of your victims end up your loyal slaves. Lay out the perks and limitations of this macabre ability.

### Recipe #159 – Sniper Surprise

1 - #You are (or were) a spy, with a superhuman skill set.

2 - You've got a mystical distance weapon that inflicts superhuman damage. Feel free to merge any of your other powers with it.

3 - You can create short-ranged teleportation portals, through which you can spy/attack/flee/maneuver.

4 - The second your firstborn draws breath, you'll stop aging and cannot die—until your last descendant dies. This could also apply to beings you create or "turn" (say, with a vampire's bite).

5 - You have access to a reliable network of allies within business, government, and other legitimate sectors of society. Set the details.

### Recipe #160 – Sonic Tikka

1 - #Your sonic attack inflicts sound-based and kinetic-force damage. Is it a yell, weapon, or something else? Feel free to merge it with other (relevant) powers/weapons.

2 - Your lungs allow you to carry a note/scream/breath attack for several minutes and even hold your breath for hours at a time.

3 - #You can't feel emotions of any kind. Boost either your Intellect or Will attribute to superhuman capacity.

4 - You can detect and listen in on any sonic frequency.

5 - You have a number of lesser powers, which must be inspired by one of your other abilities.

### Recipe #161 – Soul Scalper Alfredo

1 - You can put your victim's soul into an object (like a weapon, amulet, or coin). Anyone it touches can tap into that soul's memories, skills, or powers—pick one and set the details.

2 - You can put someone's deceased soul into a different corpse (and resurrect it). Feel free to merge this power with other (relevant) abilities.

3 - #You're playfully insane—until angered. Also, your mind's immune to mental intrusions of any kind. Boost your Endurance, Will, or Intellect to superhuman capacity.

4 - You can use weapons with a skill that's beyond superhuman. Feel free to merge another power(s) with this one.

5 - For better or worse, your name is feared far and wide. Set the pros and cons of having such an infamous rep.

### Recipe #162 – Sourdough Getaway Driver

1 - #You are—or were—a professional villain. Pick up a criminal skill specialty that you can utilize, with superhuman capacity.

2 - You have a unique, feature-loaded vehicle (from a spy car to a missile to a star cruiser).

3 - Whenever you're in a dangerous situation, you'll have unnaturally good luck—until the crisis ends. Then your luck returns to normal.

4 - Your skill's beyond superhuman when driving or flying a vehicle—even for the first time.

5 - You have an extensive network of reliable criminal contacts.

### Recipe #163 – Spaghetti Alpha Vamp

1 - #You're a truly evil monster who must feed upon the living to survive. Boost two of your human-scale attributes to superhuman capacity.

2 - You can convert other beings into whatever you are (and pass along powers, skills, weaknesses, etc.). Anyone you train/turn is inclined to obey you.

3 - With a bite and direct "tasting" of a target's blood, you can turn him/her/it into your loyal slave for months at a time.

4 - #While you may take damage normally, only a handful of things can truly kill you. Boost your Will, Endurance, or Health attribute to superhuman capacity.

5 - #Whether you're a genius or just pretty quick-witted, you often make very good decisions—to the point where people tend to follow you.

### Recipe #164 – Speedster Stew

1 - #You're a speedster, which allows you to move at superhuman capacity (possibly faster than sound).

2 - You can do hundreds of small actions per second (from trigger pulls to punches to fast-building something). What are the limitations?

3 - You have a form-fitting field of solid air that's invisible to the naked eye and protects you from most attacks.

4 - #You're a genetic superhuman (born or augmented) with one free power and one superhuman attribute.

5 - You can safely exist in most hazardous environments.

### Recipe #165 – Spell Gangster Danish

1 - #You can cast spells. Boost your Will attribute to superhuman capacity.

2 - You have a useful network of mystical contacts.

3 - #You're meaner than most people. Boost your Endurance and Will attributes to superhuman levels.

4 - #You are—or were—a professional villain. Pick up a criminal skill specialty that you can utilize, with superhuman capacity.

5 - You have an extensive network of reliable criminal contacts.

### Recipe #166 – Split Personality Crepes

　　1 - #You have some kind of symbiote within your body (biological, psychic, tech-based, mystical, etc.). Feel free to merge your other power(s) with it.

　　2 - You have (at least) one split personality.

　　3 - You can temporarily copy the innate psychic powers of those around you—as long as they stay within your power's range.

　　4 - You know the precise location of every living thing around you.

　　5 - You can temporarily copy the innate organic (non-psychic) powers of those around you—as long as they stay within your power's range.

### Recipe #167 – Scrambled Power Vendor

1 - #You're a remarkable kid. How is up to you. Pick one attribute and boost it to superhuman capacity.

2 - #Each day, at least one of your other innate powers will randomly (and uncontrollably) turn into some other innate power.

3 - Pick another ability and multiply its range or count (but not duration) to your advantage.

4 - You can make one of your other powers' (temporary) effects permanent.

5 - You can give a copy of one/more of your other powers (and optional weaknesses) to another being. How does that work?

### Recipe #168 – Star God Antipasto

1 - #You're a fledgling/lesser god, who can (to some extent) bend reality on a whim.

2 - You have an extensive network of extraterrestrial contacts.

3 - #Your Speed, Endurance, Might, and Health attributes are at the superhuman level. You can also self-regenerate by the minute.

4 - You've got an indestructible (mystical) item/weapon that'll return to you from anywhere. When using it, any feats you make are in the superhuman range. Any powers you merge with it will go beyond superhuman capacity.

5 - You're an expert in almost everything alien, with a skill level that's beyond superhuman.

### Recipe #169 – Steamed Sisterhood

1 - As long as you're working/fighting alongside allies, your side will always beat the odds. Why?

2 - #You're a well-versed killer. Your talents can be merely human or at superhuman capacity.

3 - You have a one-of-a-kind, non-mystical weapon. You can wield it with superhuman skill. Its material strength is beyond superhuman capacity. Set the other details.

4 - As long as you're moving around, incoming attacks tend to miss you. This power works at superhuman capacity—even on attacks you don't see coming. Of course, some attacks can't be dodged.

5 - #You are stunningly attractive and/or charismatic, which allows you to convince people to do what you want.

### Recipe #170 – Storm Curry

1 - #You're a powerful minion who answers to Nature itself, via the element of wind. Pick up two extra powers that will help with your duties.

2 - #You have a superhuman flair for finding people and solving mysteries—whether you're a spy, lawman, freelance sleuth, or someone's pet enforcer.

3 - You can control the weather. Set the range and other details for this power. Feel free to mix this with other (relevant) powers.

4 - You can hover (or outright fly) on currents of air.

5 - Pick one of your other powers and permanently amplify it beyond superhuman capacity.

### Recipe #171 – Storm Junkie Saltimbocca

1 - Somehow, your innate powers were raised beyond superhuman levels. However, you also have a number of irritating weaknesses.

2 - You can control the weather. Set the range and other details for this power. Feel free to mix this with other (relevant) powers.

3 - Merge this ability with any area-effect power/weapon you have. When using it, you can spare anyone or anything within its range (but nail everyone else). You just have to know where your "friendlies" are first, for this power to work.

4 - You have a form-fitting field of solid air that's invisible to the naked eye and protects you from most attacks.

5 - If knocked out, any powers you had in play might remain active for a while longer (perhaps long enough for you to regain consciousness).

**Recipe #172 – Story Dragon Quiche**

1 - #You're a full-blooded dragon. Aside from the wings, enhanced attributes, armored scales, and a breath attack, add the little perks and flaws.

2 - #You can copy the appearance and voices of other humanoid beings.

3 - As long as your legend survives, you can't age or stay dead.

4 - For better or worse, your name is feared far and wide. Set the pros and cons of having such an infamous rep.

5 - You can turn into any non-mystical animal.

### Recipe #173 – Sugar-Free Gianthood

1 - #You can grow to a certain height. Set the details (both for yourself and anything you have on you). If you want to be permanently large, that's fine too.

2 - Any damage you sustain from mystical attacks is reduced to human capacity.

3 - You can share some/all of your innate powers with everyone within a certain range. That could suck if you're surrounded by friends and enemies. The effect ends when you cut it off, get separated, or lose consciousness.

4 - During a fight, you'll be able to ignore your injuries (from broken bones to fatal wounds) until the fight's over—then it'll all catch up to you. Do note: certain injuries will still kill you on the spot (like decapitation or a nuke blast).

5 - #Whether you're a genius or just pretty quick-witted, you often make very good decisions—to the point where people tend to follow you.

### Recipe #174 – Summoner Fondue

1 - #You're a world-class expert in the occult, with secrets worth killing for.

2 - You're well-versed in summoning mystical creatures (from other planes of existence).

3 - Bad things happen to those who break an agreement with you. Feel free to mix another power(s) with this one.

4 - This power allows you to talk to beasts and (usually) control them.

5 - You can contact beings in other dimensions.

### Recipe #175 – Summoner's Puppet Butterscotch

1 - #Your permanent handicap boosts one of your other powers beyond superhuman capacity.

2 - You're well-versed in summoning mystical creatures (from other planes of existence).

3 - You have the loyalty of a very dangerous being. Assign this individual three powers and a backstory.

4 - You can control a living target's body, like one would a puppet.

5 - From miles out, you can establish two-way telepathic contact with a handful of minds. Feel free to merge this power with other relevant abilities.

### Recipe #176 – Sumo Tots

1 - #You're built like a sumo wrestler—with superhuman Might and Endurance.

2 - For better or worse, your name is feared far and wide. Set the pros and cons of having such an infamous rep.

3 - You can teleport (with one passenger) across a certain range.

4 - Your skin's hardened against both physical and mundane energy attacks.

5 - You can heal from most injuries within a few minutes.

### Recipe #177 – Super Gangster Dumplings

1 - #You are—or were—a professional villain. Pick up a criminal skill specialty that you can utilize, with superhuman capacity.

2 - You have a skill with automatic weapons that's beyond superhuman.

3 - You have access to a loyal group of combat-hardened minions. Give them gear and an origin story (hired mercs, temporary conjurations, members of your tribe, etc.).

4 - You have a high-powered firearm of some kind, which does superhuman damage.

5 - You can heal from most injuries within a few minutes.

### Recipe #178 – Surfer Calzone

1 - You can move through the water disturbingly fast, for hours at a time. Hopefully, you have some way to breathe underwater.

2 - #You can turn into a living mass of liquid. If you wish this to be your permanent state, that's fine too.

3 - Somehow, you can shoot a powerful stream(s) of water. How this works is up to you.

4 - You can shoot razor-sharp shards. What one material are they made of? Set the details. Feel free to mix this power with any others you might have.

5 - #You have an overwhelming need to do good—even if you're a benign crook. Boost two of your attributes to superhuman capacity.

# The Antagonists' Cookbook, Vol. 1

### Recipe #179 – Tac Vest Gumbo

1 - #You've mastered a non-mystical fighting style, which allows you to fight with superhuman capacity.

2 - You have a small arsenal of offensive and/or defensive gear.

3 - Any clothing you wear has a superhuman toughness, until you take it off.

4 - Whenever outnumbered in a fight, you (somehow) take way less damage than you should—even if fighting dozens-to-one. Why is this?

5 - Your insults (no matter how trite) attack the mind with superhuman ability. Those who can't resist will have their actions "jinxed" so badly that their feats are at human scale.

### Recipe #180 – Techie Salad

1 - #You're a cyborg, to the point where most of your body's been replaced with artificial components. Feel free to mix your other powers into this one. Are any of your attributes increased?

2 - Your weapons, implants, and/or gear have safeguards against theft, sabotage, tampering, disarmament, etc.

3 - You can turn parts of your body into small devices. Set the details and limitations. Feel free to merge another power(s) with this one.

4 - #You are (or were) a spy, with a superhuman skill set.

5 - You have some kind of variable-yield ammo (or possibly a power), which allows you to inflict different types of damage on a target. Examples would be gadget arrows, specialized bullets, or even assorted eye beams.

### Recipe #181 – Technopath Au Gratin

1 - #You're a well-versed killer. Your talents can be merely human or at superhuman capacity.

2 - You can remotely hack into computers (via psychics, magic, or a bit of both).

3 - You have a small arsenal of offensive and/or defensive gear.

4 - You have a weapon that fires sensor-filled projectiles.

5 - You can send and receive communications signals over vast distances.

### Recipe #182 – Telekinetic Basilico

1 - You can move solid objects, either via telekinesis or some kind of tractor beam.

2 - You have a form-fitting field of solid air that's invisible to the naked eye and protects you from most attacks.

3 - You can disarm your foes with a skill that's beyond superhuman.

4 - Your mind has some kind of defense against psychic attacks, which functions at superhuman capacity.

5 - #You're a super genius with a number of non-violent skill masteries (set the details). Boost your Intellect to superhuman capacity.

### Recipe #183 – Temporal Gangster Cake

1 - #You were born in a vastly different time period (past or future). Set the backstory.

2 - You can open a portal to any point in the past or future.

3 - #You're part of a hive mind. Set the details. Feel free to merge another relevant power(s) with this one.

4 - You have access to a loyal group of combat-hardened minions. Give them gear and an origin story (hired mercs, temporary conjurations, members of your tribe, etc.).

5 - You have an extensive network of reliable criminal contacts.

### Recipe #184 – Temporal Pocket Rolls

1 - You've got a secret lair, with sufficient resources to pursue your objectives (whatever they may be).

2 - You have a secret lab with the resources to pursue your field(s) of study.

3 - You can open a portal to any point in the past or future.

4 - You have a useful, chatty object (like an implant, ship's AI, or talking mage's staff). Feel free to merge your other (relevant) powers with it.

5 - You have your very own pocket dimension. Assign the rules, perks, and drawbacks to such a place.

### Recipe #185 – Toasted Nanoswarm

1 - #You're some kind of robot. Boost three of your attributes to superhuman capacity.

2 - #You can turn into a being of (what seems to be) hard-hitting smoke. Set the details, perks, and limitations.

3 - You can turn parts of your body into small devices. Set the details and limitations. Feel free to merge another power(s) with this one.

4 - You and/or your gear have a superhuman resistance to radiation (from EMP attacks to spatial radiations to dental X-rays).

5 - If you consume metal, while injured, you'll heal by the second.

### Recipe #186 – Tox Shot Assortment

    1 - You have a chemistry skill that's beyond superhuman capacity.

    2 - You have armor-piercing projectiles that can pump a desired drug/toxin into a target.

    3 - You have some kind of variable-yield ammo (or possibly a power), which allows you to inflict different types of damage on a target. Examples would be gadget arrows, specialized bullets, or even assorted eye beams.

    4 - You have a secret lab with the resources to pursue your field(s) of study.

    5 - Your skill with pistols is beyond superhuman capacity.

### Recipe #187 – Trigger-Happy Venison

1 - You can create man-portable, modern-day weaponry out of thin air. Feel free to merge another power(s) with this one.

2 - Your attack feats are beyond superhuman capacity when using paired distance weapons.

3 - #You can cast spells. Boost your Will attribute to superhuman capacity.

4 - Your distance attacks will harmlessly pass through the first solid object they hit (like a wall or body armor), then turn solid again. Set the details.

5 - You can leap up, down, and across great distances. Even if your arm strength's human, your kicking strength's superhuman.

### Recipe #188 – Tuna Dream Spy

1 - You can enter and control the dreams of others. Can you brainwash or even kill people within their dreams?

2 - You can generate an area-effect pulse of superhuman capacity. Anyone who can't resist it will fall into a deep, natural sleep.

3 - With this power, you can establish a one-way mental contact and copy some/all of a target's memories to your own.

4 - If attacked while unconscious, your body will either fight or flee (until the threat's done). Then you lose consciousness (until you'd normally wake up).

5 - #You are (or were) a spy, with a superhuman skill set.

### Recipe #189 – Two-Headed Cobbler

1 - You have extra heads attached to you—each with its own brain and independent personality.

2 - You've got a focused beam attack that sucks life energy away from your target. Feel free to mix this effect with another power(s).

3 - You have hundreds of skills in your head (maybe more).

4 - You have a number of lesser powers, which must be inspired by one of your other abilities.

5 - #Whatever you are, you can't pass for a human. Boost two of your human-scale attributes to superhuman capacity. Set the details on what kind of creature you are.

### Recipe #190 – Undercover Performer Ham

1 - #You're a versatile musician-songwriter with a skill that's beyond superhuman.

2 - Touch a corpse and you'll have its every memory and skill.

3 - #You've mastered a mystical fighting style. That's why your fighting and acrobatic abilities are at superhuman capacity, along with your striking damage.

4 - You can convert other beings into whatever you are (and pass along powers, skills, weaknesses, etc.). Anyone you train/turn is inclined to obey you.

5 - You can create regular (or customized) archaic melee weapons out of thin air. Feel free to merge other powers with this one.

### Recipe #191 – Vamp Tarts

1 - Any offspring you have will grow to full maturity within a matter of hours. Set the details on how this happens (alien DNA, magic, genetic flaw, etc.).

2 - #You're a truly evil monster who must feed upon the living to survive. Boost two of your human-scale attributes to superhuman capacity.

3 - Somehow, you can make liquids move (pretty much) however you want them to.

4 - You can impregnate a living victim and expect one/more offspring within a number of hours. The rapid gestation will probably kill the host. Set the details on how this happened (sex, monster bite, mystical curse, viral sting, etc.).

5 - You have hundreds of skills in your head (maybe more).

### Recipe #192 – Vampire Samurai Biscuit

1 - #You're a predatory creature with unique dietary needs—but also some good left in you. Boost your Will and two other attributes to superhuman capacity.

2 - As long as you're moving around, incoming attacks tend to miss you. This power works at superhuman capacity—even on attacks you don't see coming. Of course, some attacks can't be dodged.

3 - #You have extensive military experience and a natural affinity with any kind of weapon. Also, boost one of your attributes to superhuman capacity.

4 - You have a one-of-a-kind, non-mystical weapon. You can wield it with superhuman skill. Its material strength is beyond superhuman capacity. Set the other details.

5 - Establish eye contact and you can hypnotize a target(s) at superhuman capacity.

### Recipe #193 – Vampiric Crystalline Pie

1 - #You can turn into moving, living crystal. Boost two of your attributes to superhuman capacity. Set the details (including whether or not this is your natural state).

2 - You can teleport a number of beings (as a group) over a certain range.

3 - You can emit a blinding light that doesn't affect you at all.

4 - You've got a focused beam attack that sucks life energy away from your target. Feel free to mix this effect with another power(s).

5 - You can maneuver and fight by sound alone.

## Recipe #194 – Vegan Sidekick

1 - #You've mastered a non-mystical fighting style, which allows you to fight with superhuman capacity.

2 - You can heal from most injuries within a few minutes.

3 - You can throw non-weapon objects with a skill beyond superhuman. Whatever you can lift is fair game—from baseballs to lamps to crowded buses.

4 - You're able to make distance attacks that move/bounce around obstacles to hit a target. How does that work?

5 - You always find whatever you need to achieve your objective(s). Too bad having the right tools doesn't guarantee success.

### Recipe #195 – Walnut Demon Blades

1 - You've got a mystical melee weapon that inflicts superhuman damage. Feel free to add any of your other powers to it.

2 - You can safely cross into other dimensions (with decent odds of safe return).

3 - You have a spare weapon or piece of gear. Thus, you have a matching set. Feel free to merge one or more of your other abilities with this one.

4 - You can hold spirits within you and (try to) tap into their collective abilities, memories, and skills. Set the pros and cons for this scary power.

5 - #You've got demonic blood in you. Pick up one extra power and boost two of your attributes to superhuman. Now, what kind of demon are you?

### Recipe #196 – War Prophet Scampi

1 - #You have accurate visions of the future. Set the details and limitations.

2 - You can survive dangers and heal from anything within a day—as long as you don't have any kids.

3 - Stand in a particular place and you can look into its past.

4 - #You are stunningly attractive and/or charismatic, which allows you to convince people to do what you want.

5 - You have access to a loyal group of combat-hardened minions. Give them gear and an origin story (hired mercs, temporary conjurations, members of your tribe, etc.).

### Recipe #197 – Whisked Exorcist

1 - You can hold spirits within you and (try to) tap into their collective abilities, memories, and skills. Set the pros and cons for this scary power.

2 - #You're an anointed follower of a higher (or darker) power. Boost either your Will or Intellect to superhuman capacity. Needless to say, your prayers tend to get answered quickly (but in strange and mysterious ways).

3 - You know how to do exorcisms (whether by ritual magic, a mystical object, innate power, or some other way).

4 - #You're a world-class expert in the occult, with secrets worth killing for.

5 - You can change the moral alignment of others, at superhuman capacity.

### Recipe #198 – Whole Grain Techno Dwarf

1 - #You have enough dwarven blood to get the perks/limitations. What are they?

2 - #You're a cyborg, to the point where most of your body's been replaced with artificial components. Feel free to mix your other powers into this one. Are any of your attributes increased?

3 - Your battle armor protects you from damage and raises your Might attribute to superhuman capacity. What other features does it have? Feel free to merge another power(s) with this one.

4 - You have a secret lab with the resources to pursue your field(s) of study.

5 - Whenever using a hand-held distance weapon, you'll never run out of ammo.

### Recipe #199 – Winged Freak Dijon

1 - You've got some kind of wings, which allow you to fly. Feel free to combine another power(s) into this one.

2 - You can turn invisible to all forms of detection (the five senses, psychics, tech, and even magic). Set the details and limitations.

3 - You have a noticeable organic armor that's permanently bonded to you (like a shell).

4 - You have some kind of variable-yield ammo (or possibly a power), which allows you to inflict different types of damage on a target. Examples would be gadget arrows, specialized bullets, or even assorted eye beams.

5 - #You can temporarily grow a bit taller and sprout extra muscles. Boost your Speed, Endurance, Might, and Health attributes to superhuman capacity. Set the details (including duration) and feel free to merge another power(s) with this one.

### Recipe #200 – Zookeeper Pork Pie

1 - This power allows you to talk to beasts and (usually) control them.

2 - You can create animals out of thin air.

3 - You can make living beings (but not yourself) grow to massive heights.

4 - You can call upon animals to save you (as long as they aren't already trying to kill you). How's it work?

5 - #Your skills at wilderness combat, survival, and tracking are at superhuman capacity.

## ABOUT THE AUTHOR

**Marcus V. Calvert** is a native of Detroit who grew up with an addiction to sci-fi that just wouldn't go away.

His goal's to tell unique, twisted stories that people will be reading long after he's gone. For him, the name and the fame aren't important. Only the stories matter.

You can find his novels, anthologies, and writing guides at:

*Website:
https://www.talesunlimited.net

*Twitter:
https://twitter.com/MarcusVCalvert

*TikTok:
TalesUnlimited Marcus V. Calvert

*Facebook:
https://www.facebook.com/TalesUnlimited

## CURRENT TITLES

Short Story Anthologies

The Unheroic Series

*Unheroic, Book 1*
*Unheroic, Book 2*

The Book Of Schemes Series

*The Book Of Schemes, Book 1*
*The Book Of Schemes, Book 2*
*The Book Of Schemes, Book 3*

Novels

I, Villain Series

*I, Villain*
*Murder Sauce*
*Frag Code*
*Coin Game*

Writing Guides

The Batchery Series

*Batchery, Volume I*
*Batchery, Volume II*
*Batchery, Volume III*

The Antagonists' Cookbook Series
*The Antagonists' Cookbook, Vol. I*

Made in the USA
Monee, IL
01 April 2022